TALES FROM THE
SCAREMASTER™

WEREWOLF WEEKEND

TALES FROM THE SCAREMASTER™

WEREWOLF WEEKEND

by B. A. Frade
and Stacia Deutsch

Little, Brown and Company
New York Boston

Copyright © 2016 by Hachette Book Group, Inc.
Text written by Stacia Deutsch
Cover illustration by Scott Brundage
Tales from the Scaremaster logo by David Coulson
TALES FROM THE SCAREMASTER and THESE SCARY STORIES WRITE THEMSELVES are trademarks of Hachette Book Group.

Little, Brown and Company

Hachette Book Group
1290 Avenue of the Americas, New York, NY 10104
Visit us at lb-kids.com

Little, Brown and Company is a division of Hachette Book Group, Inc. The Little, Brown name and logo are trademarks of Hachette Book Group, Inc.

The publisher is not responsible for websites (or their content) that are not owned by the publisher.

First Edition: September 2016

ISBN 978-0-316-31623-1

10 9 8 7 6 5 4 3 2 1

RRD-C

Printed in the United States of America

*Don't make the same mistake
Emma made. Don't read my book.*

—The Scaremaster

Chapter One

"Remember the time we were at the amusement park and the ride got stuck?" Sam asked as we walked up the middle school steps.

"And we were there for an hour..." I added, adjusting my backpack straps as we went.

"And you started singing that hilarious song..." Sam hummed a few notes.

"Hang on," I interrupted. "Do you hear that?"

"What?" Sam cupped her ear.

I closed my eyes and listened. Beyond the normal morning sounds of the school buses in the distance, mixed with teachers' voices that drifted down the hallway, I distinctly heard a low-pitched whine.

"Is that a cat?" I asked, stepping back from the door to let some other kids pass by.

"I don't think so," Sam said. I could see the

scientist inside her perk up. "Come on, Emma. Let's find out."

The first bell rang, which meant we only had ten minutes to investigate. I didn't mind being late to school, but that wasn't Sam's style. If she thought ten minutes was plenty of time, I was with her.

"Let's go," I agreed.

We hurried back down the steps and toward the wild, untended bushes on the far side of the bus drop-off, by the sports field. The bushes were so thick, and filled with thorns, that we all knew never to reach in there. Any balls that were lost were lost forever.

That was where the whine came from.

"What do you think it is?" I asked Sam. My own imagination was flipping from cat to rat to three-headed toad to screaming banshee. I had a really good imagination. In my head, anything was possible.

Sam was more rational. She listened to the whine and ran through the database in her head before answering, "Dog. Small dog. Terrier, maybe."

I bent down near the source of the sound. She was right. "It's a puppy," I said, seeing the little white furball tangled among the thorny branches. It really was a terrier. The cutest one I'd ever seen, with big brown eyes and floppy ears. She wasn't dirty or matted. It was clear that this wasn't a stray or a dangerous animal: This was a lost dog that needed to go home.

"What do we do?" I asked again, my brain jumping from calling the fire department to digging a tunnel.

Sam set her heavy backpack on the ground and took the scissors from her pencil kit. I had a pencil kit too, but mine just had pencils and a few pens. Sam's had "supplies." Using those sharp scissors, she cut through the brambles until the puppy was free. It bounded out of the bushes and leapt into my lap.

Sam bent to read the dog's tag. "Her name is Maggie." She giggled as Maggie's long pink tongue popped out and licked her face. She wiped her cheek with the back of her hand and said, "There's a phone number."

Taking turns carrying her, we took the puppy to the school office and arrived, just as Sam had predicted, with plenty of time to make it to class. We even had time to wait while Principal Robinson called the number on the tag and spoke to the old man who answered. We could hear his excitement through the phone.

My heart soared as I hurried into my first-period class. We'd saved a puppy and helped an old man. It was a great start to the day.

I thought that with such a great start, maybe Mom would change her mind, so I texted her. She texted back. And just like that, the best day became the worst.

Chapter Two

"She's ruining my life!" I dropped my head to the table and gave a mighty groan.

Sam put a gentle hand on my shoulder. "Your mom probably doesn't mean to ruin your whole life, Emma. Just this one weekend."

"Yeah." I peeked up at her with one brownish-green eye, my lid partially closed, and my mouth formed into a scowl. "Easy for you to say. You're going to have the best weekend ever." I sat up, keeping the scowl. "Starting in a couple hours, you get to spend three days with your cousins. I have to spend those same days with Mrs. L!"

"Ugh." Sam shuddered as a chill went down her spine. "I didn't realize that was the actual plan. I thought you were kidding. Oh, Emma, you're right. Your mom *is* ruining your life."

"Exactly," I said, flopping forward again until

my head banged against the lunch table. My long brown hair covered my face and muffled my voice when I complained, "I can't imagine anything more horrifying."

Mrs. Langweilg was my upstairs neighbor. Mom called her "quirky," but that was wrong. "Weird" was a better choice. Her crowded apartment was hoarder weird, she smelled funky weird, and her obsession over her ferret pets was creepy weird.

Nope. There was nothing "quirky" about Mrs. L.

"I wish your mom would let you hang out with us this weekend," Sam said for about the millionth time since I had told her Mom was going away on business. "It's going to be an epic sleepover."

"I bet that's why she said no." I kept my head down. "She talked to your mom and found out that your parents are also going away for the weekend."

Mumbling to the floor like this, I found that I was looking at the bottom of Sam's boyfriend jeans, staring at her ankles, which were sticking out of her bright red sneakers. Sam's dad was black and her mom was white, and I was struck by how pretty a shade of brown her ankles were. Ankles…

this is what my weekend had come to. All I could think about were my neighbor's ferrets and Sam's ankles. It was depressing.

"It's only two nights, and they aren't going far," Sam told me. "Just to a fancy hotel downtown. It's my mom and her twin sister's twentieth high school reunion. That's why the cousins—"

"Augh!" I moaned even louder than before. "Don't remind me!"

I couldn't believe Mom was forcing me to spend the weekend with Mrs. L instead of sleeping over at Sam's. I'd never met Cassie and Riley, but if they were anything like Sam, I was going to miss out on something truly amazing.

"Maybe you can use Mrs. L as a character in one of your stories," Sam suggested as a way to cheer me up.

"Maybe..." I said, considering the idea. I really like writing stories. I usually have a pen and some paper nearby for when I get inspired. I'm the only twelve-year-old in Madisonville Middle School who is published. Last summer, I wrote a horror story about a severed head that lived in the middle school gym. It was published in an online magazine.

"Nah," I said at last. " 'The Langweilg Nightmare' is a story I don't want to write."

As I closed my eyes, though, the story started forming in my head. It went like this:

After school, I change out of the brown leggings and patterned sweater I was wearing and put on an old, ugly T-shirt with baggy sweatpants instead.

I am on my knees, scrubbing the stains off the old lady's bathroom floor while Mrs. L is in the other room, sitting in her creaking rocking chair, knitting booties for those creepy pet ferrets.

The horrifying vision repeated itself, with me crawling on the floor in the kitchen, in the hallway, and across the bedroom.

Ewww.

I push away any thoughts of where those goopy stains might have come from in the first place. They are everywhere! And they never really go away—no matter how much I clean.

I shuddered.

This was a pretty exact description of how it had gone last time I spent a weekend upstairs. When I told my mom, she thanked me for being so kind to our elderly neighbor. She was so proud of me, blah, blah, blah....

I guess some stories are better left untold.

"Emma...Yo, Emma..." Sam gave me a shove. "Anyone home?"

"Huh?" I looked up.

"I've been talking to you for like five minutes. Did you hear anything I said?"

"No. Sorry. I was just thinking...."

"Your brain is a mystery that science will never understand," Sam said, gathering the trash from her lunch.

"I'd say the same about yours." I grinned.

"Come on. I have an idea." Usually, Sam wore her dark curly hair in a tight ponytail. Now it was loose and wild. I've always believed that Sam's hair could predict the future—the more it frizzed out, the more fun was on the way.

This was max frizz.

"During recess, I'm going to get some things together and plan activities for the cousins. You can help!" she told me.

That didn't sound fun at all. It sounded terrible. Planning things I couldn't do...

"No thanks," I told her. I hadn't eaten any of my lunch, so I stuffed the unopened paper bag in my backpack and stood up. "I probably should get a head start on my homework. I'm gonna spend recess in the library."

"Oh." Sam looked longingly outside the big window in the middle school cafeteria. There was a huge banner over the exit announcing the middle school winter dance in a month. And a poster for softball tryouts. If I had to pick between them, it would be dancing. I couldn't throw or catch to save my life.

Sam slung her backpack over her shoulder. "The library sounds great. I'll go with you. I'll find a new book to read."

"Don't you have a stack of books next to your bed?" I asked. Sam was always reading at least two different books at the same time, sometimes three or four. My brain was busy, but hers was busier— in a different way.

"I've been branching into astronomy." She smiled. "There's going to be a full moon this—" She cut herself off before she added "weekend."

"It's okay, Sam," I told her. "You don't have to feel sorry for me. I'll meet you in class."

"Are you sure?" she asked.

I nodded. I was grumpy and didn't want to drag Sam down.

She headed outside with some of our other friends while I went through the thick glass library doors, past the computer stations, straight toward the first empty desk.

"Emma?"

I had just finished my assignment and turned to see a woman standing at the librarian's station. I didn't know the school had hired a new librarian. Our usual librarian was ancient. Mrs. Frankle had been my mom's librarian when she was in middle school. This librarian was young. Pretty. And somehow, she knew my name.

"Where's Mrs. Frankle?" I asked quietly. I hoped she wasn't sick, or worse...fired.

"Oh, she'll be back." The librarian gave a small shrug. She had straight hair that was so dark it was practically purple. Her eyes were the same color as her hair. Or maybe they weren't. I couldn't tell.

They seemed to keep changing. "What's going on, Emma? It looks like you're having a rough day."

I turned my head away, confused. Was I supposed to know her name like she knew mine? Should I ask her who she was? Should I pretend I knew her? This was awkward.

I studied a dirty spot on my tennis shoes while I considered what to do.

"You seem unhappy. Would you like to talk about it?" she asked. I felt like she already knew what was going on with my mom, Mrs. L…with everything.

I didn't look back up. "Not really." I quickly added, "But thanks."

"Sometimes the best listener is a book," the librarian said, coming around from the station. "Writing in my journal always helps me get my head in order." We always whispered in the library, but she was talking even softer than a whisper. I strained to hear her. "Do you keep a diary?"

"No," I whispered back. "I only make up fictional stories. I never write about myself." Even if I did write "The Langweilg Nightmare," I'd create a character that wasn't me. I found that storytelling came easier when it wasn't personal.

"Today's a good day to make a change." She flicked her purple-black-brown-green-gold eyes toward a nearby rolling cart. There were spiral notebooks on the top shelf above the books that had recently been returned to the library. "Take one."

I didn't want to be rude, so I went to take a look. Even if I didn't use it as a diary, I could always use a new blank book.

She returned to the library desk and stood there while I decided. The librarian stood statue still, patiently looking at me, sort of staring, but not exactly. Those odd eyes seemed to bore through me, seeing me and, at the same time, looking at something beyond my head. I could feel their heat even as I turned my back to her and studied the book cart. I struggled to stay focused.

Most of the notebooks were the spiral kind, like the ones everyone buys the first day of school for class. They were in all colors and sizes. I ran my fingers across the metal bindings, pretending like I was trying to decide.

As I came to the end of the row, there was a book that stood out from the others. It was thicker and didn't have a spiral binding. Instead, it had a weathered brown leather cover with a small brass locking clasp. Etched into the front cover was a geometric design made entirely of similar-sized triangles in a deep golden color. There were so many triangles, they covered the entire surface, even peeking out from under the clasp.

There was no doubt that this was a special journal. I immediately wanted it.

"Can I really take one of these?" I felt like I needed to double-check with the librarian. She pushed up her glasses before responding, which made me wonder if she'd been wearing glasses when I first came into the library. I didn't think so.

"Yes," she said with a sweep of her hand. "Whichever one speaks to you."

That was a funny way of saying it.

I thought about asking specifically if she meant I could have the leather journal instead of one of the office-store kind, but she was no longer looking at me. She suddenly seemed busy; the phone was tucked between her shoulder and ear while she read something on the computer.

I told myself that since the leather one was with the others, she must have meant that one too.

"Thank you," I said, a little louder than I should have. She responded, not by saying "Shhh," but by pointing to the clock above the librarian's desk.

Recess was nearly over. I had to get to class.

I put the journal in my backpack and took off through the glass doors and down the hallway.

Chapter Three

"Did you get a lot of homework done?" Sam asked, plopping into the desk next to mine with a whoosh. She dropped her backpack on the ground between our desks. It clanked.

"What?" I had almost forgotten why I'd gone to the library in the first place. "Oh, yeah, I did." I glanced at her backpack. "What's in the bag?"

"During recess I began 'collecting' things from school for—" Sam stopped herself. "I'm so sad you can't come over."

"Good afternoon, class." Mr. McCarthy entered the room.

My conversation with Sam ended because Mr. McCarthy began collecting book reports. It didn't really matter what Sam was planning with her cousins. It was probably better not to know, since I wasn't going to be there anyway.

"Please take out paper and a pencil," Mr.

McCarthy said, pushing up his thick black glasses. "We're going to do some free writing. The topic for this assignment is 'My Plans for the Weekend.' "

I wanted to scream. He had to be joking!

First, we had to write about ourselves, which I didn't like doing. And second, we had to write about the weekend, which, for me, wasn't going to be fun at all.

I considered writing a Cinderella sob story about a teenaged girl scrubbing the floor with her toothbrush. But I couldn't do that. I'd get a zero for not doing the assignment correctly.

Resigned to writing a pathetic paragraph about myself, Mrs. L, and the ferrets, I reached into my backpack for a sheet of lined paper.

My hand brushed the leather journal. I felt a small electric shock, like after scooting on carpet in socks and then touching something.

I paused. Shook the feeling off. Then dug deeper in my bag. I had put in a new pack of lined paper before leaving home this morning. Where was it?

The back of my knuckles leaned against the journal as I bent over to sort through my stuff. That odd shock I'd felt before felt more like a magnet now. My fingers felt heavy against the journal, and I had this sensation that if I'd only turn my hand around, to face it with my palm, it would leap into my hand.

I rotated my wrist, and sure enough, the book seemed to lean into my palm. And with that was the strong sensation of wanting to take it out of my bag. I felt like I desperately wanted to write in that journal. Right now. Right here.

And why not? There was nothing stopping me.

The new librarian had suggested I start a diary. And Mr. McCarthy wanted a personal essay. He never collected free writing—just looked at it in class—so I wouldn't have to give up the book. I let it fall into my hand.

Yes. I could do two things at once: start the diary and do the assignment. Now seemed as good of a time as ever to crack the first page.

I set the journal on my desk and carefully bent back the cover. The pages inside weren't white or lined. They were yellow, like the yolk of an egg, and the paper was thicker than regular paper. I ran my hand over a page, feeling the roughness, then, on impulse, bent down to smell it. The journal smelled woodsy: damp dirt and fresh pine mixed with smoky campfire. When I sat back up, the scent of wet dog lingered.

The book seemed like something from an antique store. I wondered why the librarian had been so willing to give it away.

Closing my eyes for a second, I imagined myself writing with an old-fashioned quill, instead of a plain old number two pencil. I let the image fade, then got started. At the top of the first page, I wrote:

My Boring Weekend

I underlined it twice for emphasis.

Uncertain what to write next, I leaned back in my chair.

I'd never had a problem getting started, but now I felt all blocked up. With this fancy journal lying across my desk, it felt like I needed to say something important. Something interesting. The pressure was on, and the words weren't flowing.

I chewed on my fingernail and glanced over at Sam, who always complained about free-writing assignments. She was already feverishly filling the second side of a page and working so furiously that she'd probably fill three more before I even began.

With a deep breath, I decided to dive in.

Dear Diary,

I guess I should call you that.

I can't believe that Mom is leaving me behind again! What did I do to deserve another weekend of bathtub scrubbing and ferret socks????

Okay, that wasn't so hard. I wondered why I'd always resisted keeping a diary. All I had to do was write down what I was feeling. My emotions poured out onto the page: mad, disappointed, annoyed…left out. I quickly filled one page and turned to the next.

Mr. McCarthy was wandering the room, helping students who were stuck. I hunched over my work so he wouldn't think I needed him, because I didn't. I was writing faster and with more emotion than ever before.

So, to sum it up: My plans are to have the most boring weekend in the history of the universe. While Sam gets to have the best weekend ever. Life is so unfair!

Pausing my pencil, I couldn't help glancing over at Sam, who was obviously describing in detail her own amazing weekend plans. Sam raised her head, smiled sympathetically at me, then continued on a new page.

I looked back at the journal, quickly rereading what I'd written. When I got to the bottom of the page, I gasped.

"Whoa! What? How the—" I didn't realize I'd spoken out loud until I noticed that the entire class was staring at me.

"Is something wrong, Emma?" Mr. McCarthy asked, eyebrows wrinkled with mild concern.

"No. Nothing," I muttered, but my heart was racing. "Just getting into the assignment."

"All right. Keep your thoughts to the page, then, okay?" he said with a smile.

I nodded as he turned away to help Duke Garcia, the new kid who'd just moved into the house next door to Sam, retrieve his crutches.

Sam kept her eyes on me. "What's up?" she mouthed.

"Nothing," I repeated, and looked back at the journal.

Right under where I had written *Life is so unfair!*, in a scratchy scrawl that was somehow cooler than my own handwriting, a reply had appeared:

Unfair, you say?

A familiar shiver went up my spine. The kind that comes when I'm reading something scary, which I do a lot to get in the mood to write my own stuff. The feeling usually comes during the first few pages, where everything seems so "normal," but in the pit of my belly I know something dreadful is about to happen...and keep happening.

Sam doesn't understand why I like that feeling. She could read the same stories as me and have a thousand reasons why "whatever" could never happen. These are some of our best late-night discussions.

It's hard to explain to someone practical and grounded how a burst of adrenaline pumping in your head is enjoyable, but it is—enjoyable. Usually.

Today, not so much. From the moment I saw someone else's writing in the journal, I was feeling like a spring, wound up and ready to pop. *Where'd that writing come from?*

I pinched myself to make sure I wasn't asleep. Okay. I was definitely awake.

I shut and rubbed my eyes, fully expecting that when I opened them, the extra words would have disappeared. But when I peeked back at the page, there was even more strange, scratchy writing.

The Scaremaster doesn't want you to have a boring weekend. You started the story, and now I will finish it. My way!

"Augh!" I jumped up from my desk, knocking over my chair. Lightning fast, I slammed the journal shut and threw it into my backpack.

Chapter Four

My pencil clattered to the floor and rolled to where Mr. McCarthy was standing. He bent low and picked it up.

"I believe you dropped this," he said, walking slowly over to my desk. I could hear snickers echoing around the room as I tipped up my chair and sat back down at the same time that he returned my pencil.

My face felt red, and my mind was racing. All eyes were on me, and I had to focus on the most important pair. Mr. McCarthy stood over me for a long beat, then asked the same question he'd asked before. "Is something wrong, Emma?"

"No. Nothing," I said in a rush of breath. The room was blazing hot.

The concern I'd seen in his eyes when I'd first interrupted class had turned to suspicion.

"I need to see your assignment," my teacher said. With a meaningful sideways glance, he told the class to get back to work and mind their own business. I could actually feel their curious heat shift away from me.

"I finished it," I told him. "All packed up and put away." I gave him a small, stressed-out smile.

"Take it out, please," Mr. McCarthy said. He gave me a stern look over his glasses.

"No thanks," I replied. "It's really good. You can trust me. I have big plans for the weekend."

"You do?" Sam cut in. "I thought you couldn't come over because of ferret-sitter?"

"Exactly. Ferrets are fabulous." I glared at her, hoping she'd get the point. I didn't want to take the journal out of my backpack. That thing was possessed, and until I could get it away from school, I had to keep it closed. "I love ferrets." I quickly added, "And their little-bitty socks."

I couldn't show anyone the journal. Nobody would believe that those words had just appeared. Certainly not my mom. She would think I was working on a new story. Even *I* wondered if I had made up what had just happened....

Sam would be the worst one to tell.

My best friend was a bit of a mad scientist. Whatever she was collecting at school—I had no doubt it was for an invention or experiment. Sam was grounded in exploring reality and for sure would never believe in an ancient-looking, supernatural, possibly demonic book that could write back.

I had to figure out what was going on...and I had to do it on my own.

I glanced down at the journal in my bag. If there was a way to get out of class, I could just take it back to the library and pretend nothing unusual had happened today. But Mr. McCarthy was blocking my direct path to the exit. Plus, he was still waiting for me to hand over the journal.

He held out his hand impatiently, and I stalled, thinking about what to do. The truth was...I didn't want to give up the book. Not yet. There was a part of me that was curious. A part of me that wanted to know why that book felt like it belonged to me. Why, of all the journals on the rack, I had picked that one. Why it shocked me— and why it wrote to me. I wasn't making this stuff up, and like Sam the scientist, I wanted to find out the reasons.

One thing was certain: I wasn't touching that thing again before I had a chance to come up with a strategy...and that would take longer than I had at this moment.

Too much time had already passed since Mr. McCarthy had asked for the book.

I tapped my fingers on my desk, looked up at Mr. McCarthy, and gave him a huge, albeit fake, grin. "So, uh, what are *your* plans for the weekend, Mr. McCarthy?"

He didn't answer my question. Raising one eyebrow, he said, "Show me the journal."

I shook my head.

He pointed to my backpack. "I'll have to give you a zero...."

That ended the debate. I had no choice.

"Oh, fine," I gave in. I pulled the book out of my bag, part relieved and part confused when it didn't shock me this time. Without a word, I handed it over and didn't dare to breathe as he opened the cover to the first page.

He read silently.

My blood was racing. I felt hot. Sweaty. And cold. With chills.

Then, after what seemed like forever, he closed the cover and handed the book back to me with a laugh. "What a creative way to approach the assignment." Mr. McCarthy had a small Santa belly that shook as he chuckled. "Keep up the great work."

And with that, he moved to the other side of the room, where Genevieve Lee had a question.

I studied the book. What had made Mr. McCarthy laugh like that? Why wasn't he freaked out? There were so many questions spinning in my head.

Moving with extreme caution, I raised the edge of the cover, peeked under the leather binding, and turned to the first page.

"Huh?!" I whispered it this time, but the room was so quiet that the entire class turned to look at me yet again.

I ignored their stares.

My words were gone! Every pencil mark. Every period. It was as if the book had reset itself.

Now, on that same yellowed page was a title. It said:

Tales from the Scaremaster

And below that, the story began, in handwriting that looked a lot like mine.

Once upon a time, there was a girl named Emma....

I quickly shut the book again, shoved it deep into my backpack, and sat there, nervously tapping my foot on the floor until, finally, the bell rang. I had to get through two more periods before I'd have time to investigate—and maybe by then I'd feel calm enough to open the journal again. I told myself to act normal. Act like nothing interesting was going on. It was going to be a long afternoon pretending that I didn't have a talking book in my backpack, but I could do it....

Sam and I were on our way out of class when Mr. McCarthy stopped me. "Hey, Emma, I didn't know you kept a journal."

I was calm. Cool. Perfectly normal. "Just got it today. Thought I'd explore keeping a diary." I gave him a big grin because everyone knows that teachers love students who do extra, unassigned work at home.

"It's a nice book. Unique," he said. "Where'd you get it?"

I decided to be honest. "The new librarian gave it to me."

His expression was odd. "We don't have a new librarian. I saw Mrs. Frankle at the staff meeting this morning."

"Are you sure?" I asked. There was a sinking feeling in the pit of my stomach, like I was at the top of a roller coaster, about to drop from the highest point. What was going on? No new librarian? "Maybe it was an assistant?"

"I don't think so."

And with that, my mental roller coaster went over the edge, and I was in a free fall. My stomach flipped over, and I felt wave after wave of nausea.

"Are you sure?" I asked, one last-ditch effort. Maybe he was confused. "Mrs. Frankle was here this morning as in today—*today, this morning*?"

"I'm positive, Emma." Then, as if he had better things to do, my teacher said, "Well, time to get ready for the next class. Enjoy the journal, Emma. Happy writing!"

He pulled out a folder and began reviewing his notes. For him, the conversation was over. For me, it had just begun.

Sam was waiting for me at the door to walk to science together.

"What did McCarthy want?"

As she asked it, I blew past her, down the hall, running like an Olympic athlete into the library. I was out of breath, heart racing, brain on overload, when I shoved open the doors to find...

Mrs. Frankle sitting at her desk.

"Hello, Emma," she greeted me. "Can I help you find something?"

"Where's the new librarian?" I asked in a voice that was way too loud. "The young one with the funky eyes."

"I'm the only librarian here," she said in her library voice. "Yesterday, today, and always," she added with a throaty chuckle.

"Where's the cart?" I rotated on my heels to look for the cart with the journals. It was gone.

"What cart?" Mrs. Frankle said, coming to me. "The book cart has been broken for a month. A wheel fell off, and it's not in the budget to fix it." She was clearly concerned about me. "Sweetie, are you all right? Should I call your mother?"

"During recess today, there were journals on a

cart right there!" I pointed to the empty spot near her desk.

My voice was so loud she put a finger to her lips. "Shhh." Then she whispered, "No, there weren't. I've been here all day. No cart. No journals. No new librarian." Mrs. Frankle put the back of her hand on my forehead. "Hmmm. I don't think you have a fever. But to be certain, I think I should walk you to the nurse."

I lowered my voice and assured her, "I'm okay. I had a bad dream last night about the library and came to check it out." I pinched my lips together and added, "Must have been my imagination."

Mrs. Frankle laughed and pushed up her glasses, which I realized were the same ones the other librarian had been wearing! "You're just like your mom. She had a big imagination too. I used to have to warn her not to read scary stories before bed." She put an arm around me and walked me into the hall. "Say hello to your mom for me, won't you?"

"Yeah. Sure," I said absently while I looked deeply into Mrs. Frankle's eyes. She probably thought I was staring, but I had to see what color they were. The answer was brown. Just brown, no flecks of any other color.

But the glasses...

I pulled myself together. "I'd better go. I'll tell my mom what you said."

Chapter Five

That whole "investigate this on my own" thing I'd come up with in English class didn't seem so good on the way home. What if the book was really possessed? What should I do then? What did possessed books want? I didn't know what to do, but with every question, I got more and more scared.

I needed advice. Since Sam wouldn't believe me anyway, there was only one other option. She was going to have to dust off her rusty, hardly-used-anymore imagination, but I had no doubt once she did, she'd know I was telling the truth and want to help.

I burst into the apartment like I'd been shot out of a cannon. "Mom! Mom! Mom! Mom!"

"Whoa, slow down, Emma." Mom was bent down behind the door. When it flung open, the knob nearly rammed into her ear. Luckily, she jumped back in time.

"Mom, you aren't going to believe—" I dropped my backpack on the floor. "I can't explain. I just have to show you." I knelt down on the floor beside her and reached into my bag for the journal.

"Emma, I really don't have time right now." That was when I saw that she was leaning over her suitcase. I hadn't really processed why her head was so close to the doorknob, but now I understood. The zipper on the old bag was stuck, and she was hunched down, struggling to get it closed.

She was leaving.

I sighed.

Mrs. L was probably waiting for me upstairs. There was no way I was going to show that old bat the mysterious journal. She'd probably want to use the pages to line her ferret cages.

"Mom, I have something to—"

"Help me out here, Em." Mom looked so frazzled, I left the journal in my bag and sat down on top of her suitcase. She easily tugged the zipper closed. "Thanks," Mom said, then pointed to my room. "Go pack."

"But I—" I really wanted to show her the book before she left. Deep inside, there was a part of me that thought once she saw it, she'd stay home.

"There's been a change in plans," Mom told me. She ran to the bathroom and grabbed her hairbrush. I waited for her to explain while she ran it through her dyed-red hair. We used to look more alike until she started messing around with the color. Of course, I still have her straight, sharp nose and slightly oversized ears if someone really cared to look.

"Work called. I have to leave earlier than expected," Mom said, tying her hair up into a bun, which only emphasized the Glick-family ears.

My shoulders slumped. "Oh," I said.

"And Mrs. L can't take you."

"Did you say 'can't'?" My eyes widened. "As in 'cannot'?"

"One of her ferrets had to go to the vet hospital. She just told me. It was very sudden," Mom explained.

"That's too bad," I said sarcastically, wondering where this was going.

"I worked everything out with Sam's mom." As she said it, my heart jumped in my chest. "I'm going to drop you off on the way to the airport. You'll have the whole weekend with Sam. Won't that be fun?"

I didn't want to jinx it, but I had to ask, "And the cousins?"

"Yes. Riley's only ten, but Cassie is sixteen. I figure if Mr. and Mrs. Murdock think Cassie is old enough to watch Sam for two nights, then she's old enough to watch you too."

"Great!" No more questions. No more stalling. I had to get packed before she changed her mind or Mrs. L called to say her ferret had recovered and she was going to be home after all....

I made it to my room in four seconds and was ready to go in less than a minute.

"Do you need your backpack?" Mom said, with one last check that the stove was off and the lights out. "Take it if you have homework."

"Oh, right." Homework...HA! Whatever I hadn't finished at school could wait. I would finish up Sunday night when I got home. I decided to leave my pack—and the journal—behind. Mom and I could investigate it together later. Maybe by then whatever disembodied spirit was living in the pages would have moved on to a new home. Mrs. L might like someone to talk to....

As we walked out the door, Mom asked, "Did you want to show me something?"

I smiled. "No. It wasn't important. I...I...I just wanted to tell you that Mrs. Frankle says hi."

Mom dropped me off. She wanted to talk to Mrs. Murdock, but Sam's mom had run to the store for a few last-minute things and wasn't back yet.

"I'll check in later, then," Mom said, and gave me a big "I'll miss you" kind of kiss.

As she got into the car to leave, Sam and I did a happy dance and she whispered, "I thought your mom was ruining your life."

"I was wrong." I had goose bumps as a flash of Mrs. L's goopy goo went through my imagination. "She's not ruining my life. By leaving me here, she's saving it!"

I waved good-bye one last time as Mom drove away.

We'd barely gotten inside when a cab pulled up in front of the house. It wasn't one of those normal-sized taxis. It was a big van.

Sam grabbed my hand, dragging me back outside, toward the van. "Come on, Emma. Cassie and Riley are here early! Come meet them."

I had to jog a little to keep up.

The cousins didn't get out right away, so we hung back as the driver began piling luggage on the sidewalk.

"Wow," I said to Sam. "They sure come with a lot of baggage." I looked at my own little tote. "I hope I have enough clothes."

Sam laughed. "If you need more stuff, just take what you want." For years, Sam and I had been sharing clothes. We had the same casual style, meaning we weren't the best dressed at school, but we weren't the worst either. She added, "Half the stuff in my closet is probably yours anyway."

Sam lurched forward when Cassie got out of the van, but then pulled back again because Cassie wasn't ready to be welcomed. She was arguing with the taxi driver. From the bits I could hear, she was mad that he wasn't careful enough with a massive wooden trunk she'd brought. I could see her eyes flitting from the driver to the trunk and back again.

There was something aggressive about the way

Cassie stood, hands on hips, chest puffed out. If I were the cab driver, I'd have apologized, told her that the ride was free, offered to pay for the damage, and fled. But he wasn't me, and he wasn't going to give up the fare that easily.

While they fought it out, Sam and I waited.

After what seemed like a really long time, Cassie and the cab driver settled their differences. Only then did Sam's cousin Riley climb out of the backseat, hauling two overstuffed backpacks. Sam had told me that Riley sometimes modeled kids' clothing for catalogs, and I had to admit, she was adorable. Cropped blond hair, carefully styled. She was wearing a short dress with leggings and boots. I had to smile. Riley was better dressed, with way more fashion sense than me and Sam together.

Cassie, on the other hand, looked like she was about to join a death metal band. Or rob a bank. She was wearing all black. Black jeans with a black shirt and a black belt, and not surprisingly, her hair was black as well. So deeply black, in fact, it reminded me a little of that young school librarian I had met today. The one who might or might not have existed.

"Is Cassie a vampire?" I whispered to Sam, who totally didn't get the joke.

"Huh?" She gave me a sideways glance.

I shrugged and pretended I hadn't said anything at all. Instead, I pointed at the house next door. Sam lived on a quiet tree-lined street with historic houses. Sam's house was old but had a hip antique vibe. The house next door, on the other hand, looked like the model for a haunted house, with ivy and vines covering the front. It had been empty for years and would need a lot of work to get it up to the neighborhood standards. Movement caught my eye.

That new kid at school, Duke, was peeking out between the thick red living room curtains. Sam spotted him too. When he saw us looking at him looking at us, he quickly closed them.

"I think you scared him away," I said to Sam.

"Not me," she countered. "I'm not scary. You are. . . ."

"Nu-uh," I teased.

We went back and forth like that a few times like preschoolers, until we both started laughing.

Finally, we turned our backs on Duke's creepy house. It was time to greet the cousins.

"Hey," Cassie said as the taxi pulled away. She had her eyes pinned on Sam, without giving me as much as a glance.

Sam leapt into Cassie's arms. "I am so happy you're here!" Sam cheered. "Where are Aunt Alice and Uncle Bernie?"

"At the hotel. They're meeting your parents there later for the reunion," Cassie said.

It seemed strange to me that Cassie and Riley had come alone in a cab. My mom would never have let me go anywhere in a taxi by myself. Then again, maybe things would be different when I was sixteen. I really hoped so.

Moving from Cassie to Riley, Sam gave her little cousin a bear hug and then a high five. "Wait until you hear what I have planned!" Sam told her. "We are going to have so much fun." She tugged me forward. "Meet Emma," she told the cousins. "She's my best friend."

Cassie looked at me as if seeing me there for the first time. "I thought it was just us," she said to Sam. "You know, the cousins." She lowered her voice and said, "We haven't seen each other in a few months. I thought we were going to catch up."

"We are going to catch up!" Sam didn't seem to feel the negative vibes I was getting. "Emma's cool," she said, but I immediately knew that I was not welcome, by Cassie at least.

Riley was the opposite. She popped forward, and instead of a handshake, she hugged me around the waist. Her hair smelled like roses. She not only dressed better than I did, she smelled better too. "Hi," Riley said, looking up at me with a big grin. "Can we be best friends too?"

"Sure," I said. "I can have two best friends." I glanced over at Cassie, wondering if there was any chance that we could be friends as well. I hoped she'd realize I hadn't meant to crash whatever she had planned.

Riley let me go, and I approached Cassie, wondering if I should hug her or shake hands, but she kept her arms crossed. So I crossed mine too.

"Emma, right?"

I nodded. "Hi."

"We're going to carry this trunk inside." It wasn't a request. It was a demand.

I looked over at Sam, but she seemed oblivious to Cassie's attitude. This wasn't the cousin Sam had described. The writer inside me wondered what her story was. Had she changed from the way Sam remembered?

"Riley and I will take the other bags," Sam announced. "We're going to sleep in the living room so we can all be together. I have sleeping bags and pillows and a Nature Channel documentary to watch before bed!"

A Nature Channel documentary...that was so Sam. I would have laughed if Cassie hadn't been staring at me with those huge brown eyes of hers. She looked so serious. I hoped she wasn't going to ruin Sam's fun.

"Let's take everything to my room," Sam said as she and Riley headed into the house, each carrying two suitcases plus a backpack.

I hefted the trunk by one handle while Cassie took the other. The leather straps cut into my hands. "What's in here?" I asked. "A dead body?"

"No," Cassie said, but didn't react to my joke.

"Did the cab driver complain the trunk weighted down his car?" I asked with a smile, trying again.

"No," Cassie said simply.

"Was—" I gave up my questions. She'd only say "no" anyway.

We moved slowly, step by step, into the house. Crossing through the living room, I stepped toward the stairs leading up to Sam's room.

"No," Cassie suddenly blurted.

"I didn't ask anything," I told her, wiggling

my hands around a little. My fingers were getting numb.

"I knew you were going to ask about going upstairs," she told me. "The answer is no. The trunk goes in the basement."

There was nothing in the basement. Just storage and spiders.

I opened my mouth to tell her that, but she shot me a look that clearly said "Don't ask. Don't argue." So I clamped my lips shut.

Very slowly, we hauled that trunk through the narrow basement door and down the steep stairs.

"Over there." Cassie instructed me to set it in a far corner under a dimly glowing lightbulb swinging on a wire. I was very careful so I didn't get yelled at like the cab driver.

"Whew," I breathed when I stood up. Things were off to a strange start. I was anxious to get to Sam's room and let the fun begin.

Without waiting or asking about my rough red hands, Cassie walked past me to the stairs. When she reached the landing, she flicked off that lightbulb. I distinctly heard her say, "I don't know why you came this weekend. It's going to be hard enough to keep Sam from finding out. I need you to leave. As. Soon. As. Possible." And then, more quietly, "Before it gets too dangerous."

With that warning, she shut the door before I was even out of the dank basement, leaving me alone.

I wasn't usually afraid of the dark, but there was something terrifying about being left in it after being lectured about how you weren't wanted. I put my hands out to feel the side walls, and I stepped cautiously up each step. Every time a floorboard creaked, I shivered. That familiar feeling was back again. Dread with a touch of fear settled in my stomach.

I'd seen enough horror movies and read enough scary stories to know this was only the beginning.

Chapter Six

I walked into Sam's room to find that Sam had already handed out schedules for the weekend. They were on computer-printed stationery that had the image of the moon across the top.

One of the things Sam loved about science was the order and predictability of it all. Her room was so organized I never wanted to touch anything. Colors were grouped, books sorted by author's last name, and everything was in its place.

Her schedule was highlighted. The times marked in yellow. Activities in blue.

She was sitting with the cousins on the floor, reviewing the pages.

It was as if nothing strange had happened.

I wanted to ask Cassie what she had been talking about in the basement, but the way she was acting made me wonder if I'd imagined it. She was happily chatting with Sam about dinner plans.

I stood in the doorway until Sam noticed me there.

"What took you so long?" Sam asked, as if I'd been gone for hours.

There was no good answer for that one. I could have said something snarky like "Please tell Cassie that it's impossible to lock someone in a basement with no door lock." The other option was to tell the truth: "Your creepy cousin ditched me in the basement, and it took me a little while to navigate the last few steps in the pitch-black."

It was too early to cast a judgment, but it seemed to me that Cassie had two personalities: one for Sam and a different one for me.

I wasn't sure that complaining about my version of Cassie was the best way to go, so I changed the subject. "What did you get at school today?"

"I got an A in science....Oh!" She laughed at her misunderstanding. "You mean what did I get during recess?" She picked up her school pack from next to the small desk. Tipping it over, Sam poured out the things I'd heard clank in class. She quickly put the items in an organized pile.

"I have a big metal tube, glue, scissors, electrical tape, a piece of cardboard...." she rattled off the list. "I got the pipe and the tape and the other stuff from Mrs. Popski, the janitor." She waved her hand at the stuff on her desk. "Mr. McCarthy gave me the rest after school."

I hadn't seen Sam after school. I was in too much of a hurry to get home and tell my mom about the book. Thinking about it, I felt a strong surge of relief that the *thing*, and whoever/whatever lived inside it, was far away from here.

"I got these on the Internet." Sam opened her drawer and pulled out two glass discs. "One concave and one convex." She looked past me to Cassie and Riley. Cassie was scrolling through her phone, but Riley was interested. "Want to guess what we're making?" Sam asked her.

"A microscope?" she asked, coming over to get a better look at the supplies.

"Nah. But close." She looked at me as if I knew.

"A telescope?" I asked. It was the glass lenses that gave it away.

"Yes! For tomorrow's full moon!" Sam exclaimed, handing me a copy of the schedule and catching me up. "We're going to do all kinds of things this weekend to celebrate astronomy. In the morning, we'll bake moon pies, then build a telescope. Tomorrow night, we'll check out the moon, eat the pies, and take a moonlit walk."

There was other normal sleepover stuff detailed in the schedule too, like taking selfies, watching online videos, and the whole "sleeping in the living room" part, but it was the moon stuff that I was excited for.

Moon-related activities might not sound fun to everyone, but I'd been her best friend long enough to know whatever Sam wanted to do was going to be amazing. She could make waiting for leaves to change color into something fascinating.

"Tonight, we'll just hang out," Sam said. "And watch that documentary I told you about."

Sam loved the Nature Channel. I wasn't that into it, but she usually chose things that kept my interest. Thanks to Sam, I knew more than the average middle schooler about beekeeping, the Arctic Circle, and sedimentary rocks.

"Is it about the moon?" I asked.

"You betcha," Sam said. Her eyes glittered with pure joy.

"I can't wait…." It was then I realized that

Riley and Cassie hadn't said anything about Sam's big Saturday-o-fun. I turned to look at them. They'd moved over by the doorway, where Cassie was whispering to Riley. She nodded. Cassie whispered some more.

"So," Cassie addressed the rest of us. "I think we can do some of that tomorrow," she said, not committing to the entire day-evening schedule. "But Riley and I have different plans for tonight." She crossed to one of her two suitcases and opened a pocket on the outside. "I brought her favorite movie." Riley took it and passed it to Sam. "Do you have a DVD player?"

"Sure," Sam said. "Lots of stuff I like to watch is still only on DVD." She held up the box. "*Closer Encounters of a Different Kind.*" The back read, "Interviews with teenagers who have had close contact with werewolves, vampires, and zombies."

"It's a documentary," Riley said proudly. "Just like your moon one."

I could have guessed what Sam was going to say.

"This is fiction," she snorted. "Not a documentary."

She tossed the box to me. I missed it, of course, and it slid on the carpet, stopping at Riley's feet.

"I like it," Riley told her, scooping the box up and holding it to her chest. "And I say it's all real."

"Aren't you too old for that kind of made-up nonsense?" Sam asked. "Vampires and werewolves don't really exist." She added, "Neither do zombies."

"You don't know that for sure," Riley said, casting a quick glance at Cassie.

I saw the look that passed between them but was pretty certain Sam missed it.

Sam asked her cousin, "Cassie, do you believe in supernatural beings?"

"Of course," Cassie said.

It was on the tip of my tongue to joke again about how she dressed like a vampire, but I held back, swallowing hard. Instead, I asked Riley, "Doesn't this stuff scare you?"

"Nah." She shook her head. "It actually makes me feel better about stuff."

I felt an immediate connection with this girl who loved horror like I did, but at the same time, I wouldn't say watching something scary made me feel "better." It made me feel tense, anxious, edgy....

"It calms her down," Cassie added, with another quick look to Riley. "That reminds me," she sort of said to us, but more to herself, "I'll be right back."

Cassie was on the way out when Mrs. Murdock stuck her head in. She had her hair up in two pigtails and was wearing her weathered high school spirit jacket. After some warm hugs and "My, how you've grown!" exclamations, she said, "All right, kids. Unfortunately, there's no time for chitchat. I'm leaving. Everyone else is already at the hotel. I'm running late as always!" She rubbed her hands together. Sam and her mom looked so much alike, just like me and my mom used to—before she discovered the magic of the beauty parlor. "I can't believe we've been planning this weekend for a whole year. And here it finally is. I'm excited to see all our old friends!"

Sam groaned as her mom gushed a little about her days as a cheerleader.

Mrs. Murdock finally said, "Cassie, you're in charge. If you need anything whatsoever—call."

"Of course." Cassie grinned in a way that made me nervous. Her mouth seemed to be smiling, but her eyes were narrowed and her teeth gnashed together.

I shut my eyes and counted to three. My imagination had been on fire ever since that creepy book spoke to me at school. It was a growing list of weirdnesses: first the journal; then the trunk; now Cassie's attitude, secretive glances, and awkward grins.

I told myself to relax. I was acting ridiculous— just on edge from the whole journal fiasco. Nothing strange was going on. I was wrong about Cassie trying to chase me out of the house. If I gave it time, we'd be friends.

I said all that to myself, but I didn't believe any of it.

Right after Mrs. Murdock left, Cassie went to do whatever it was that she'd forgotten. I moved downstairs with Sam and Riley to the living room. It was early still, so we'd agreed to watch both movies. Vampires, werewolves, and zombies before dinner and moon landings after.

We settled into the couch, surrounded by pillows and blankets. Cassie still wasn't back from whatever she was doing when Riley put in the disc.

"Press play, Sam. It's okay. My sister's seen this one a thousand times," she told us. "She knows it by heart."

I settled back on the couch, determined to enjoy the movie. I wasn't like Sam. I wasn't 100 percent negative about the existence of werewolves or vampires, but to call the movie a "documentary"... well, that was a stretch.

The movie began with a fake-looking news report about a boy who had encountered a teen vampire in a dark hallway at his high school. There was a really quiet part where the boy paused dramatically in his story, pulling back his long brown hair to reveal two puncture wounds in his neck, directly above his collarbone.

"He tried to turn me," the boy told the camera. "But I escaped." There was dramatic drumming music. Then he said, "This is my story."

Cassie still hadn't come back when the vampire segment was over.

In the transition between the vampire interview to a different kid who claimed he had seen a werewolf, I heard a banging sound. I jumped.

"What was that?" I asked Sam.

"Huh?" She was only half watching, flipping through a book about the solar system at the same time.

"Did you hear a clanking, banging rattle?" I asked.

"It's just the radiator." As she said it, I heard the noise again.

"There it is!" I said.

"Old house, remember? We hear stuff like that all the time," Sam said, then turned the book to show me a photo of the moon's craters. "Did you know the moon is three thousand four hundred seventy-six kilometers in diameter?"

Another clank. No reaction from Sam.

I didn't think it was the radiator.

"Did you hear that?" I asked Riley, but she was too engrossed in the film to respond.

"This is a good part," she told me. "Watch, Emma. The werewolf is going to jump out from behind that tree! See, what John doesn't know is that the werewolf is actually his best friend's brother. He looks normal most of the time... except for one night a month, of course." She put a hand on my knee. "Here he comes. It's a little scary, if you want to hold hands."

I decided to skip out on the tree-popping were-wolf and go investigate the sound I kept hearing. "I can't watch," I told her. "I'll have bad dreams." It wasn't true. Mrs. Frankle said scary books kept my mom up, but I was a good sleeper. Nothing kept me up.

"But Billy is a nice boy," Riley told me, adding softly, "It's not his fault." She immediately went back to watching the film.

Another clanging sound caught my attention.

"Be right back," I told Sam and Riley, though neither of them seemed to hear me. Riley was into the movie, and Sam was into her book.

I was pretty sure the sound came from the basement, so I went straight there.

The door was cracked open.

Moving very quietly, I pushed the door wider and went down the first few steps. The lightbulb was on and swinging.

In the corner, I could see Cassie's shadow leaning over the heavy trunk. I moved down one more step, careful not to make a noise.

Cassie was starting to worry me. She was too odd. Nothing seemed right.

The next time the clanking sound came, I was

certain that it was the distinct sound of metal hitting metal. Like chains.

I squinted in the partial darkness. The lightbulb above Cassie's head flickered.

She was unloading metal bars.

I watched for a long moment as she placed a long metal bar against another bar and strapped them together. Then she added more, until she'd created a wall of bars.

Whatever she was making was huge. When she raised that metal wall, connected to a metal floor, it stretched toward the ceiling. I could make out a swinging door, the stripes of the bars reflected on the cement floor, giving the appearance of a jail cell.

The clanging echo rolled through the basement one more time. Cassie moved to the side and was no longer blocking my view.

I held my breath and squinted. I didn't blink.

Oh no! No. No. No. No. No.

I backed up the stairs, as silently as I'd gone down.

I had to tell Sam!

I didn't know how to convince her, but I'd do whatever it would take. She had to believe me.

I knew what I had seen. There was no doubt in my mind.

Cassie was building a cage with chains in the basement. It was the ONLY possibility. The bars, the shadows, the chains. It all added up.

A cage. Yes, a cage, but for what? Or who?

The thing that she intended to put in there had to be HUGE!

My brain was spinning so fast, I couldn't focus. Pictures of big animals flashed through my head like a kid's zoo book: elephant, giraffe, etc....I knew none of that made sense, but I couldn't stop the flickering images long enough to really consider what else might actually go into a cage that large. My brain was grabbing at the first and easiest ideas.

Cassie had warned me earlier that things might get dangerous. And now...here was the proof.

With great concentration, I stopped trying to figure out what went inside and focused on how exactly I was going to tell Sam about this discovery.

She liked evidence, so I'd tell her there was a cage in the basement and then show it to her. What to do next, we'd figure out after.

At this precise moment in time, only a few things were clear:

This was not my imagination.

This was not a made-up story I was writing.

This was reality.

Chapter Seven

"Sam!" I dashed into the living room at full speed. "You gotta come with me! I have to show you—"

"Shhh..." She put a finger to her lips. "To my surprise, this is actually interesting. Do you know why the full moon is linked to lycanthropy?" She translated the scientific word: "That means transforming into a werewolf."

I didn't have time for this. "Sam," I breathed her name through bared teeth. I didn't want to freak out Riley. "I need to show you something."

Sam was on a roll, and I couldn't get her away. She turned her phone screen to me so I could see the website. "It's confusing. Some say it's because of the radiant energy a full moon creates."

"I thought you didn't believe in werewolves," I said. "Has Riley convinced you?"

"Of course not," Sam told me. "But there was a study in Australia that shows that more people go to the emergency room on a full moon and more people are in violent fights. Something about the moon makes people aggressive." She set the phone down. "And that's science."

"Sam, the zombie part is next!" Riley pointed to the screen. "I love this part. This kid found a book in her locker and then—"

"That's nice, Riley," I cut her off. "Sam!" I tipped my head toward the bathroom, "Can I have one minute, please?"

"Okay," she said, reluctantly getting off the couch. "I'm not sure I can find anything scientific about zombies anyway. Dead people who eat brains? Yeah, right. That's too far a stretch. How would they even do research?"

We went into the bathroom. I shut the door.

I wasn't sure how to start, so I just went for it. "Cassie is building an animal cage in the basement."

"And I'm building a spaceship in the backyard," Sam joked with a smirk. "That's my Emma... always working on the next great story. Are you going to write it up and submit to that other fiction journal you told me about?"

"No, seriously," I told her. "It's not a story plot.

I saw it." I used my hands and arms to indicate how huge the metal bars were.

"I think this whole full-moon thing is getting to you, Emma," Sam told me. She shook her head and gave me a pathetic look. "No more scary videos for you. Maybe we should skip the midnight walk tomorrow. It might freak you out." I couldn't tell if she was kidding.

"You want evidence?" I asked, my voice rising. "I can prove it. Come with me to the basement right now!"

Sam let out a heavy breath. "When we don't find anything, do you promise to relax and enjoy the weekend?" She pinned me with a hard stare. "I am worried you might be jealous of the cousins." Explaining, she said, "I mean, I am trying to include you, but you seem to have a problem with Cassie. Why don't you like her?"

"What? Me? Jealous?" I shook my head. "That's not it at all." I opened the bathroom door and peeked out. Riley was still watching the movie. She was on the edge of her seat. "I don't have a problem with Cassie. She has a problem with me. She even told me she did."

"I know my cousin. She'd never do something so mean." Sam clearly didn't believe me.

"Don't just brush this away as if it's nothing," I said, leading her to the basement door. "There is something very strange about Cassie."

"She's from the city," Sam said, brushing me off again. "Strange to us is normal there."

"It's more than that," I said. The basement door was closed. I grabbed the knob and turned.

Locked.

"Huh?" I tried again. I switched hands. Still locked.

"Sam, look!" I stepped aside and asked her to try. She did. The knob wouldn't budge. "This door didn't used to have a lock!" I pointed at the doorknob. "It's been replaced." I bent down to investigate. "Looks brand-new to me." My hands were shaking. "If that doesn't prove that Cassie is hiding something, nothing will! It's all the scientific evidence you need."

"Maybe my mom changed the knob," Sam said. "I don't know that she didn't."

I knew for sure there hadn't been a lock when I was shut in down there. But if Sam didn't believe this was a new knob, she'd never buy that Cassie left me in the basement alone.

"Let's call your mom," I demanded. "She said we could call anytime. Now's good. Ask her if she changed the knob."

"I'm not going to bug her," Sam told me. "You're being ridiculous. It might just be stuck."

To prove it wasn't, I pulled hard. "It's locked."

"Doesn't mean anything," Sam said.

"Yes," I countered. "It *means* that Cassie is hiding a giant monster cage!"

"I'm hiding a what?"

I turned around to find Cassie standing behind me. She was wearing a flowered apron over her black wear. It looked like she'd taken a job at a hipster coffee shop.

"I just came to tell you dinner's ready," Cassie said, leaving my accusation hanging in the air between us. Her voice was now the one she used for when Sam was around. It was upbeat and joyful. "I made pizza and salad." She put her arm around Sam. "Hungry, coz?"

"Starving," Sam said, wrapping her own arm over Cassie's shoulder. "Is Riley's movie over?"

"Just ended," Cassie said. She bumped me out of the way as she passed. I knew it was intentional.

Sam locked eyes with Cassie. "Sorry I missed the ending."

"I'm sure Riley will tell you all about it at dinner," Cassie said with a giggle. A GIGGLE! I had no idea she could even smile. "She loves the werewolf part, but the zombie section has this crazy twist."

Sam and Cassie began to walk toward the kitchen. I stayed by the basement door and tried the knob one last time.

Locked.

"Are you coming, Emma?" Cassie waved to me in a casual, fake-friendly way. "You don't want your pizza to get cold."

The rest of the night went just like that. Cassie was super sweet and helpful, like a normal babysitter. Or a loving cousin. I was pretty certain that was because the four of us were together. She didn't have a chance to try to chase me away.

We had a delicious dinner and then made cookies together. They were peanut butter with chocolate kisses on top.

I was on edge.

I kept waiting for something to happen. For Cassie to grow fangs. Or to excuse herself and run off to the basement. Or to suggest we go out and look for Bigfoot. That would explain the cage. But she didn't do any of that.

She was so normal, everything was fine for hours, and that's what made it all the more absurd when I started screaming.

I saw the monster at the back door before anyone else. There was a small window in the door, and his shadow filled the glass. The shadow was tall, thin, and limping with hands outstretched. The doorknob rattled as something banged into the door. Sam's mom must have left the door partially open when she rushed out of the house. It creaked and slowly slipped open....

"Zombie!" I screamed, pointing at the stiffly lumbering figure. "Run away!" To create a distraction, I grabbed a bowl of oranges off the counter and began tossing them at the shadowy form. Why I thought pelting a zombie with oranges was a good idea, I'll never know, but my adrenaline was on fire, and the oranges were the only weapons available.

I didn't even come close to hitting him. I can't throw under ordinary circumstances, and this was anything but ordinary.

"Don't let him catch you," I warned the others as I tossed the last fruit over my shoulder and ran from the room.

Acting entirely on impulse, I fled through the house and out the front door. I was standing barefoot on the lawn when I realized Sam and her cousins were standing on the front porch, laughing so hard they were crying. And behind them was the zombie. Otherwise known as Sam's next-door neighbor Duke.

My face flushed. I was so embarrassed.

"Where are your crutches?" I asked Duke, trying to pretend the whole thing hadn't just happened. I gave him an "I was joking—wasn't that funny?" smile as I passed back into the house.

"I couldn't use them and hold the box," he said. Then I saw that he was carrying a box of donuts in his "outstretched" arms.

"Makes sense." I took the box from him. "Thanks."

Sam asked, "What's the occasion?"

"I saw your cousins pull up and thought it might be nice to give them a welcome present."

The box was from a pretty famous local donut place. It had been on national TV once.

"Now you've got them, so bye." Duke scooted past me, out onto the lawn. "Gotta go."

"Thanks," Cassie called after him. Since we'd already had cookies, she added, "I'll serve them with breakfast."

Duke stared at the ground and muttered something like "You'rewelcome" as one word, then disappeared into his own house.

I felt completely ridiculous. Of course it had been Duke and not a monster. It made sense that he would come over and do something sweet. Because I knew something that Sam didn't. Duke had a huge, giant, enormous crush on her. He'd sworn me to secrecy, and I pinkie-promised not to tell her.

I'd figured it out after Sam told me that he broke his foot when he fell out of the tree outside her window. She thought he'd gone up because it was a big oak, perfect for climbing. But I have a better imagination.

Like a writer doing research for a book, I confronted him outside the boys' bathroom at school, and he admitted the truth: Duke wanted to ask Sam to the school dance, but he didn't want to ring the doorbell and have her parents answer. He said he didn't like talking on the phone. He was too shy to ask at school. Poor awkward Duke. He tried to reach her window to have a private conversation and ended up in the emergency room instead.

And now, as he'd tried yet again to make contact, I'd started shrieking at him as if he'd risen from the dead.

Oops.

Of course, Duke *had* scared me first.

"EMMA!" Sam had been laughing outside, but now she was laughing so hard I thought she might choke. "You've got to calm down." She gasped for air, while holding her belly. "No more scary movies for you!"

I tried. But I couldn't calm down. It was like my whole being was wrapped around a firecracker, ready to burst into flames at any second. Duke Garcia was a victim of my paranoia.

Chapter Eight

We all played a board game after dinner, then went into the living room to set out our sleeping bags and watch the moon documentary.

"Did you know when the moon is full, the sun, the moon, and the earth are in a perfectly straight line?" Sam asked. "And the average time between full moons is 29.53 days?" She turned the TV to the correct channel and stepped back. "I was going to do a moon trivia contest tomorrow but decided on the nature walk instead."

"Smart move," Cassie said. "I'm no moon expert."

"I have a book," Riley said. "Mom and Dad got it for me." She frowned. "They made me read it, but I forget stuff." Riley had changed into the cutest pajamas. They were pink and frilly. Not like toddler cute but sophisticated and fashionable. There was a matching bathrobe and slippers. Riley had swept back her hair to look like a movie star settling in for the night.

"I forget stuff too," I said, supporting her. "I bet if we did trivia about fashion you'd win."

Riley smiled at me, then twirled. "I'm going to be a model, a fashion designer, a makeup artist, and a hair stylist when I grow up."

"Is that all?" I chuckled.

"I might also want to be a veterinarian, but I haven't decided on that." Then she asked, "Want me to help you pick an outfit for tomorrow, Emma?"

I knew she meant that the outfit that had been rescued from cleaning Mrs. L's floors needed help. Baggy sweatpants paired with Mom's old college T-shirt weren't going to win anything at a beauty pageant. "I didn't bring much," I told her. "But you could do my hair if you want."

Riley's eyes lit up. She turned to Sam. "Can I do yours too? We can dress up for the moon celebration!"

"I'd love it!" Sam cheered. "That will make tomorrow even more special."

"How about you, Cass?" Riley was really excited. "You too? Please?"

"Riley..." Cassie started, but then stopped.

For a flash, I was sure she was about to reveal her true self, but she bounced out of it. "That sounds like a great idea."

I was on guard; she couldn't keep this nice act up forever. I'd be there when she snapped, and then Sam would believe me!

Her cousin was keeping some major secret. I just had to prove it. Scientifically. With evidence. No problem. It was going to happen.

I snuggled down into my sleeping bag. It was warm and cozy. I could easily fall asleep before the movie ended.

Sam pressed play.

Space-themed music started when Riley popped up out of her own sleeping bag. "I forgot to brush my teeth," she said. "Mom made me promise to brush them every night." She skipped toward the stairs. "And no midnight snacks!" She laughed.

Sam paused the movie while we waited for Riley to come back from Sam's room, where all our bags were stashed.

"Riley, where are you?" Cassie called up the stairs after a few minutes had passed.

"Boo!" Riley popped up from behind the couch, which made us all jump. "Gotcha!"

It was a small scare, but I jumped at least a foot off the floor. Had the whole thing with Duke not just happened, I might have pelted oranges at Riley instead. I was so on edge, thinking something was going to drop at any second. No matter how much I told myself to keep calm, I couldn't. My heart was stuck in my throat, and my legs were twitching.

In my head, I begged my heart to beat normally. I didn't want to draw attention to my nuttiness again.

Cassie and Sam laughed with Riley, so I laughed too.

"That was a good one," I said. "Yep. You got us." I added, "Ha-ha," but worried it sounded hollow.

"Look!" Riley gnashed her little white teeth together. "Aren't they shiny?" I could smell the mint. Her hands were behind her back. "I brought my new best friend her toothbrush too." She looked at me. "And I found this cool book in your bag." Riley pulled her hands out and held them in the dim glow of the TV.

It was the journal from school. I could see the leather cover and little metal clasp.

"What?!" I jumped out of my sleeping bag and grabbed it from her.

"Whoa," Cassie said, coming to Riley's side. "She was just being nice."

"But I didn't pack this!" I peeled back the cover and looked. The first page still said, *Tales from the Scaremaster.*

"I peeked inside. Emma wrote a story about us," Riley told Cassie.

"No. I didn't," I protested.

"Let's see it." Cassie held out her hands toward me. "I want to read your story, Emma."

I did not like the way she said my name. It was slow and even, like "Emmmmmaaaaaa."

I shoved the book behind my back. "I'm telling you, this isn't my book!"

Sam got up. She circled behind me but didn't try to take the journal. "Isn't that the same notebook you had in class?"

"Yes," I said. "The librarian gave it to me."

"Mrs. Frankle?" Sam asked.

"No, the other librarian."

She looked at me like I was crazy, and honestly, I felt nuts.

"I know," I said, flustered. "We don't have another librarian. Mr. McCarthy said that too. But she was there at recess and gone after class." The look on Sam's face said clearly that she didn't trust me. "She gave me this journal."

"So it *is* yours," Cassie said.

"No," I replied. "Yes." This was hard to explain. I had picked it and taken it, so... "I mean—sort of."

"I didn't mean to make trouble," Riley said, feeding off the growing tension in the room. "I found the journal next to the toothbrush. It looked like the one in my movie, so I opened it."

"That's snooping," I told her, feeling suddenly snappy, responding as if I was being attacked. "I didn't give you permission to go through my things." The instant the words tumbled out of my mouth, I wished I could take them back.

I sounded:

1. Crazy. It was my journal after all.
2. Absurd. How could there be a story in it that I didn't write?
3. Cruel. I sounded mean to Riley, which wasn't my intention.

Then there was something else that made me pause. "Wait. Riley, what do you mean it looks like the book in your movie?"

"Weren't you watching?" Riley put her hands

on her hips. I noticed that she, Sam, and Cassie were all standing around me now in a tight circle.

"I didn't see a book," I said. I mentally reviewed the vampire story and the werewolf interview. I hadn't seen the zombie one. But honestly, I couldn't remember any details. I'd been too distracted by the banging in the basement. "Which story was it in?" I asked.

Riley let out a long, annoyed sigh. "You really should have paid attention," she said. In that moment, cute little Riley, my newest best friend, turned against me. "It's your own fault you don't know. I'm not telling you anything." She zipped her lips with her fingers.

"Enough stalling." Cassie took a menacing step toward me. "Hand over the book, Emma."

Again, like with the heavy trunk, it was a demand, not a question. Dinner-making-and-cookie-baking Cassie was gone, and the creepy, mean one reemerged with a vengeance. She was bossy again, her eyes flitted from side to side, and that attitude, the one she'd had with the cab driver, oozed out. Back on the driveway, I thought I'd have given in and run away, but after everything that had happened, I felt bolder than that. I geared up for an argument.

"Can't you see?" I flipped around to face Sam. "There's something strange about Cassie."

Sam stared at me. "You're the one making trouble," she said. "Give Cassie the book. We all want to hear what you wrote about us."

"But I didn't write anything!"

They all had their hands on their hips now. They looked so similar, these cousins.

"Fine," I said, backing down with the sad realization that my instinct to argue didn't last long. "I'll give you the book. But I am telling you, whatever it says is as new to me as it is to you because I DIDN'T WRITE A STORY!"

Tales from the Scaremaster

Once upon a time, there was a girl named Emma. Emma liked to tell stories, so I am going to tell her one.

This story begins with a secret. A dark and dangerous secret.

One night, late after the moon had risen, two girls heard something rustling behind the bushes near their school. They rescued it and set it free.

But they shouldn't have let it go.

They released a monster. A monster so terrifying it was only talked about in mythology and superstition.

Once that monster was free, he

lunged out of the bushes. Teeth bared, dripping with blood.

One girl ran away, but the other wasn't fast enough.

He sank his teeth into the soft skin on her neck and bit down hard.

In the moon's glow, the girl changed into a monster just like the one she had found.

The young girl's parents wept when they realized what had happened to their child that fateful night. They spent their days searching for a cure and their nights inventing new ways to hide the truth.

They made a pledge: Until a cure was found, no one could know what had happened that night.

Now the moon was rising again. The girl had to act fast. She made a place in the basement to hide the secret. No one would know. The secret would be hidden in the darkest shadows.

The problem was Emma.

She was snooping around. Curious. Suspicious. Emma had to be stopped.

There were big things at stake. Dangerous things.

The girl was determined to do anything she could to make Emma go away before it was too late.

With a solemn vow, she swore to protect the secret no matter the cost.

Chapter Nine

"Why would you write such a horrible story?" Sam stared at me with hard eyes.

I felt like I was repeating myself, but there was nothing else I could say. "I didn't."

"You really hate Cassie," Riley said. She moved closer to her sister and took her hand. "That's the meanest thing I've ever read."

"I didn't write it," I said again.

In the TV's flickering light, it looked like Riley was on the verge of angry tears.

"Really?! Come on, Emma!" Sam was furious. She pointed at the book in Cassie's hand. "You wrote a story that is almost identical to what happened to us at school, only with evil changes."

"The story doesn't say cute terrier puppy," I tried to argue. "It says monster. And it wasn't found *in* the bushes; it was *behind* them. Plus, there's a big difference between day and night." As

I made my list, I realized that arguing about specific words was a huge mistake. It sounded even more like I had written them, since I knew exactly what the story said.

Sam didn't appreciate my snarky reply. "The story is in your book! Found in your bag! All that, plus you're the only one I know who likes to write scary stories."

I protested her list with the first thing that came to mind. "You know that I never write anything with me as a character." Well, except that one journal entry for class, but that shouldn't count because the book made it disappear.

Sam shook her head. "You say Cassie has been acting strange, but you're the one who's being weird. It doesn't take a rocket scientist to figure this one out, Emma. The werewolf girl in your story is so obviously Cassie. You don't even have to say her name— it's that clear." She leaned in toward me and said on a long breath, "You've been jealous of the attention I've given my cousins ever since they arrived."

That hurt. It felt like she'd stabbed me in the heart. I didn't mean to ruin the weekend. I didn't mean to mess things up. All I wanted was a fun time with Sam and her cousins.

Cassie gave me a look like she'd just won. She wanted me to leave, and now everyone agreed with her.

"Give me the book," I told Cassie in a voice that was so serious she didn't argue. "This journal is ruining everything!"

"A book can't write a story by itself," Sam said.

"But it did. It does...." I was so frustrated, now I was the one who had tears in her eyes. I stomped my foot and tried to tear the book in half. The cover was thick and wouldn't rip. I tried to pull out the pages. They were stuck. I tried to split them in half. "What kind of paper doesn't tear?" I muttered when they held strong. "SEE? LOOK!"

I shouted at Sam, Riley, and Cassie, "This book is possessed!"

I was panicked that Sam wasn't going to like me anymore after tonight. This was the kind of thing that broke up best friends. If Sam kicked me out now, I had nowhere to go. Mrs. L was probably still at the ferret hospital, Mom was far away, and Sam's parents were in the city.

"I knew the journal was possessed today at school," I admitted to Sam, my voice begging her to believe me. "Remember my reaction during free-writing time? When I screamed?"

"I figured that was just you coming up with good ideas," she said.

"I pretended it was nothing, but the journal was talking—well, *writing*—to me." Sam had an incredible look of disbelief in her eyes, so I pressed on. "Mr. McCarthy thought I'd written my class work in there, but I didn't. It wasn't me writing."

"That's impossible," Sam said in a cold tone. "Of course it was you."

I tried another approach. "When would I have written that story? I was with you this whole time!"

Sam paused thoughtfully, then said, "There were gaps."

"What gaps?" I huffed.

"Gaps," she said vaguely. "Minutes you weren't with me. Long enough to write a story."

I guess when I was snooping around after Cassie could count as time I was not with her, but I wasn't writing. I was stalking! Big difference. And equally bad, now that I was really thinking about it....

Sam turned away from me and went to sit on the couch. I felt like I was losing her friendship fast, and there was nothing I could do to stop it.

"Why would I write a story about Cassie? I just met her!" I said, coming to the couch. She didn't move over for me, and when I went to sit, Riley snuck under my arm and took the seat. I had to stand in front of them, like an accused criminal explaining her case in front of a judge.

"You're creative," Sam said with a shrug.

She used to admire that about me, but everything was changing.

Sam squinted hard at me and said the meanest thing she'd ever said: "I wish you'd never come over this weekend." I thought this could not get any worse, but it did. She said, "We're going to watch the movie now. You're not invited anymore."

"What?!" I sputtered. "Where am I going to go?" This was crazy.

She tipped her head toward the stairs.

Ah, I understood. I wasn't being kicked out of the house. I was being banished. Sent upstairs to solitary confinement as my punishment.

I nodded. "Okay," I said. "But I am going to prove to you this book is acting on its own. I did not write that story. The…" I looked down at the book, still open in my hands, and for the first time, I said his name out loud. "It was the Scaremaster!"

Sam rolled her eyes. Riley scooted closer to her as if whatever was wrong with me might be contagious.

I slammed the book shut and stormed past Cassie, who was standing where she'd been this whole time and still hadn't said anything.

I was at the bottom stair when I stopped. I retraced my steps back to Cassie. She was like a gargoyle, a mean-looking statue that did nothing but stare at me with those freaky eyes of hers. I leaned in tight and whispered, "No matter what you do to me...I am not leaving." I gave a little snarl to finish the thought, like a spoken exclamation point.

I rotated on a heel and stomped up the stairs, clumping as loud as I could as I went.

I opened Sam's bedroom door with a bang and kicked it shut with an echoing slam.

Then I dropped that rotten journal on the edge of the bed and flopped into her pillows, scooting back away from it. I didn't want to touch it.

None of this would have happened if the librarian hadn't told me to pick a journal. Or back even further at school—if I had just gone with Sam to get the telescope stuff, instead of going to the library! This *was* all my fault.

I was mad at myself for making a mess of everything. Mad at Mom for going away. Mad at Cassie for being so secretive. Mad at Riley for being so cute. Mad at Sam for being so logical.

I slammed my fists into Sam's pillow and kicked my feet.

The journal fell off the bed with a sound that wasn't a normal book-falling sound.

It was like a whoosh of wind through trees. And with it, there was that smell I'd smelled before: fog and pine and damp dog. But now there was also something new, and it made the hairs on my neck stand on end: blood. Not that I'd smelled a lot of blood in my life, but it was like raw meat before it goes on the grill. My hand hurt as if I was the one who was wounded, and in my imagination, I saw blood dripping on leaves. The image brought a bitter metallic taste to my mouth.

Shaking my head to push the imagery away, I looked down toward the floor. The journal had fallen open to the first page.

It was blank!

Impossible!

I grabbed the book off the floor and violently turned through the pages.

All blank.

I had to show Sam. This was the proof I needed that I'd never written the story in the first place!

I was about to dash out of the room when fresh new writing appeared.

It was the strangest thing I had ever seen.

Words, slowly, and in that same strange handwriting as in English class, started moving across the page. Like someone was writing to me from inside the book.

Once upon a time, there was a girl named Emma....

I grabbed a pen from Sam's desk and scribbled.

Stop it. No more stories.

Hello, Emma.

How do you know my name?

I know a lot of things.
Did you like my story?

No.

Why not?

Everyone thinks it's <u>my</u> story!

It <u>is</u> your story.

That's not true! I didn't write it.

There was another possibility. Maybe Cassie had written the story knowing it would get me banished? If she had already come to the conclusion that nothing she did would make me leave, this was the second-best choice.

It made sense that she was behind all this. But then again, how could she have gotten the journal from my house, brought it here, and written in it? There was no way. I erased that option.

I told the book:

It's <u>your</u> story.

I am writing the story for you.
We are a team.

I didn't want to be part of his team. But I didn't say that, so instead I wrote:

Who are you?

You already know.

The Scaremaster?

There was a long pause. I held my breath.

Yes.

Why are you doing this to me?

Doing what?

That was a big question. I was already suspicious of Cassie when Riley found the book in my bag. The Scaremaster just let everyone know that I was suspicious, or how had be said it? *Curious.*

Then again, the whole weekend plan had changed after I wrote my essay in class. The Scaremaster said I shouldn't be bored. Could he be behind everything? Or was it really me making stuff up? AUGH! I was getting a headache trying to figure out what was going on!

I considered what to do.

I had a very important question that would determine ... everything.

The Scaremaster would know the answer.

Is Cassie dangerous?

Do you think so?

Figures. I paused to consider, then wrote:

Yes.

It's your story.
We are a team, remember?

I took that as an agreement. Not the way I wanted to hear it—and that team thing was still bugging me—but still, it felt like an agreement to me.

What am I supposed to do?

No answer. I waited. Still nothing. Maybe the Scaremaster hadn't gotten the message. I tried again:

What should I do?

Ask again later.

Didn't he understand? I didn't have time to wait. In a rush of words, I scribbled:

I need you to tell me what to do NOW!

As fast as I was writing, the ink disappeared, fading to a blank page.

Come on. Help me. What should I do?!

There was no answer from the book. I sighed. I was on my own.

Chapter Ten

I shoved the journal in my overnight bag. I knew what I needed to do next. Before the night was over, I had to get back into the group. They had to accept that I was there and not leaving. Maybe they'd even want me there if I plotted my return carefully.

I sat down to think things through.

First step: Apologize to Sam.

I had to make up with her, not just because she was my best friend, but because I had to protect her from Cassie.

Second step: Figure out what Cassie's deal was. I was thinking vampire... but that might have just been because of that movie and her love for the color black. I had never read anything about vampires that wore colors or stripes or plaid. There was also that line in the Scaremaster's story that said, "There were big things at stake." Wasn't using a "stake" the way to kill a vampire? Maybe it was a pun? Did the Scaremaster have a sense of humor? I didn't know. The second step needed more clues.

Third step: I didn't have a third step yet. Maybe if I gave the journal a little rest, the Scaremaster would be willing to give me advice. He might have just gotten tired of all my questions.

Time to implement Step One.

I headed downstairs. No clumping or stomping, just regular, calm, not-paranoid Emma.

"Hi," I said from the bottom step.

All heads turned toward me. I could see something similar to smoldering fire in Cassie's eyes. Glowing flecks of anger and frustration. This wasn't going to be easy.

"I come in peace," I said with a small smile.

Sam put up a hand to block me from her view and said, "We're watching TV, and this is the most interesting part." It was a not-so-subtle way to say, "We're busy. Go away."

I wasn't leaving. I wasn't in a place to see the

TV, so I paused to listen. The narrator was talking about moon mythology, specifically why people believed that the moon was made of cheese. This was the kind of stuff I liked watching with Sam. I would have liked to listen awhile, but there were more important matters at hand.

I forced myself to look into Cassie's flickering eyes and said, "I am so sorry, Cassie." Simple. No excuses. Truth was, I couldn't go deeper than that. I didn't want to rehash the whole story about the journal or bring up the "cage in the basement" controversy. So I just left the apology in the air and turned to Sam, then Riley, and said the same thing: "I am so sorry."

The three of them glanced at each other, and I got the feeling they'd already talked about what to do if I showed back up in the living room.

Sam was the spokesperson for the group. "You can stay down here tonight," she said. "But it's not like everything is okay."

Riley stood up and added, "I don't want to do your hair for the moon party anymore, Emma."

Cassie turned to her sister and said, "It's late, and the movie's practically done. Let's finish up and go to bed." I was surprised at how mature she sounded. It was Cassie from the kitchen talking, not the Cassie who worried me.

Then Cassie looked over and our eyes met. She mouthed at me, "Go away."

I got a chill down my spine. She still wanted me to leave.

I made a decision that no matter what Cassie said or did, I wasn't going anywhere.

I went to sit on the couch by Sam. Even if she was mad, even if she hated me forever, until the full moon passed and the cousins went home, I was sticking with her like glue. I might not look like a very good bodyguard, but it would be harder to take down two of us than one. Strength in numbers. I had run away from Zombie Duke, but I wouldn't do that again. Whatever happened from here on, I was going to stay and fight. This time I wasn't going to back down.

The movie was nearly over. I'd missed the basic facts about the moon and just heard a little of the "moon is made of cheese" mythology. The next bit was a long part about people who believed there were faces or animal shapes reflected on the moon's surface. One tradition was about a man who had been sent to live on the moon as punishment for a crime. Some thought the man had changed his ways, and now he could grant wishes. He was the Man in the Moon.

I could actually feel Sam light up when the narrator explained that the faces that people think they see are actually flat spots created by smooth lava patches.

"Wow," I said to Sam, leaning in toward her. "Fascinating stuff."

"Yeah," she said, pulling away slightly.

She wasn't ready to forgive me yet, but now that I was with her, I could deal with that.

The last myth in the movie was the one that changed everything for me. It was like a lightbulb in my head.

Werewolves.

I couldn't even listen to the narrator after he said the word. My brain was spinning a million miles an hour. Faster than the moon's rotation for sure!

Duh!

We'd already talked about the full moon and why werewolves transform. It had been in the first movie—Riley's movie.

I am no detective, but the clues were piling up.

1. Cassie had seen Riley's favorite film, with the part about werewolves, a thousand times.
2. Cassie had built a big animal cage in the basement.
3. Cassie had hedged about being able to go on the moonlit walk tomorrow night.
4. Cassie had those bizarre flickering eyes.
5. The Scaremaster story had been about Cassie and a secret.
6. The book actually smelled like wet dog!
7. The Scaremaster had basically said Cassie was dangerous.

Oh! The Scaremaster! He'd know if my suspicions were correct. I had to sneak away and ask him, but I was pretty sure I had uncovered the truth.

Cassie wasn't a vampire.

She was a werewolf!

The movie ended. While everyone was settling in for bed, I knew I needed to get away. Leaving Sam seemed like a bad idea, but it would only be for a few minutes. She'd be fine. Plus, the full moon wasn't until tomorrow night, so I had time.

"Hey, Riley," I said, trying to sound like everything was awesome and my sleeping bag wasn't right next to a werewolf's on the floor. "You still have my toothbrush? I don't want to sleep with dirty fangs...." Oops. "Teeth. I mean teeth!"

"I'll come with you to the bathroom," Riley said, handing me my toothbrush and taking her own.

Ack. I hadn't really been planning to brush my teeth. I had been planning to run upstairs and consult the Scaremaster. Now I was stuck. If I wanted to get back on Riley's good side, I had to let her come with me. So I did.

After, I said, "I need to run to Sam's room to change into my pajamas."

"Uh, Emma." Riley gave me a strange look. "Aren't those your pajamas already?"

"Right." I'd forgotten that we'd all changed after dinner. For someone who'd decided she wasn't my best friend anymore, Riley wasn't going to leave me alone for a second.

"I need..." I paused. Riley and I were at the

bottom of the steps. I glanced up, where the possessed journal was tucked into my overnight bag. Then I turned my attention to Riley. On a scale of one to ten, getting Riley back on my side was a ten. Checking in with the Scaremaster was a one. Well, maybe an eight. But still less important than Riley's friendship. It could wait. If my suspicions were right, I had twenty-four hours until I had to do something heroic.

Plus, I really had to go back to Sam.

"Okay," I said, putting my arm over Riley's shoulder. She didn't shrug me off. "Let's go to sleep."

My sleeping bag was between Sam and Cassie. Riley was on Cassie's other side.

My brain felt full and noisy. I couldn't stop thinking about what was going to happen at the full moon when Cassie revealed her true self. Did her parents truly know? The Scaremaster's story said they did and that they were looking for a cure. They must have really trusted Cassie to leave her with us on a full moon.

This was so tangled. My head hurt.

I knew I needed to sleep. But I couldn't.

I thought about the cage in the basement. Maybe

Cassie planned to lock herself in to protect us. Or maybe she planned to lock us in and run free and terrorize the neighbors! Should I warn Duke?

I had a headache the size of the moon, which was 14.6 million square miles, so it was a huge headache.

There was no way I was falling asleep. I gave up trying.

Sam's breathing was now slow and steady. Riley rolled around but was out cold. I was pretty sure Cassie was asleep too, but she kept making this throaty rattle sound that I swore sounded like a growl. A growl!

That was clue number 8.

There was no longer any doubt. I had to consult the Scaremaster.

I slipped out of my sleeping bag, careful not to wake the others. I'd be back before anyone noticed I was gone.

To be sure they were all asleep, I whispered their names.

"Riley?" Nothing.

"Sam?" All quiet.

"Cassie?"

A snarl answered me on that last one.

I shuddered.

Certain that I was the only one awake, I snuck up the stairs and closed the door to Sam's room so no one would see the light. Sitting on the floor by my bag, I took out the journal.

The first page was as blank and fresh as it had been the day I got it.

Which was today.

Oh wow, had it really only been one day? So much had happened.

I took out a pen and wrote:

Scaremaster?

You called?

Is Cassie a werewolf?

What gives you that idea?

I listed my eight reasons.

Is that all?

I was getting annoyed by his "answering questions with more questions" thing, so I asked a question of my own:

Aren't those good reasons?

Maybe. Maybe not.

I considered what to write next and decided to just say what I believed:

She's a werewolf.

Long pause, then the Scaremaster replied:

I have a story for you....

I knew how it began. It was the same as the last two times.

Once upon a time, there was a girl named Emma....

I sat in silence as the Scaremaster wrote out the whole tale. It was the longest one he'd told me, taking up five whole pages. Single-spaced. Mr. McCarthy would have been impressed.

This time it sounded like I'd written it.

It started in the park.

I sat, mesmerized, as the Scaremaster wrote out the entire tale...until the ending.

The final sentences were terrifying. Horrify-

ing. Even scarier than my own severed-head story!
Scarier than anything I'd ever read.

I was shaking when...

BAM!

The window glass above me shattered.

Chapter Eleven

When I recovered from the shock and found my nerve, I hurried to look outside. Not the smartest thing I've ever done. Had I really thought things through, I would have stayed far, far away from that window. Danger was lurking all around me.

But I wasn't thinking. I was acting on impulse, and my impulse pushed me to investigate.

The whole window, it turned out, hadn't broken. There was a small, fractured hole in the middle, which made a web of shattered glass across the pane.

With blood throbbing in my brain so hard I probably needed to see a doctor, I peered out the small open spot in the glass, careful not to cut myself.

My heart was pounding against my ribs. I had a slamming headache from the throbbing. Every hair on my head was standing up by the root. I was scared. And yet my curiosity was bigger than my fear.

I squinted into the darkness. By the light of the nearly full moon, I saw a slender figure on the grass, looking up at the window, eyes wide with a horror that matched mine.

It wasn't Cassie. Or a werewolf.

To my great relief, it was Duke.

By the horrified look on his face, he clearly couldn't believe he'd tossed a rock and broken Sam's window.

And I couldn't believe it was him. It took a few minutes for my brain to tell my body to relax. We stood like that, paralyzed, staring at each other.

"Duke!" I said at last. The window was broken, but I still managed to push the frame up without damaging it further. "I need your help," I told Duke.

Once I had fully wrapped my head around him being there, I couldn't control how happy I was to see him. It was like someone had thrown me a life vest in a rocky sea.

"Oh, it's you, Emma." He sounded so disappointed. "I thought you were Sam. I saw the shadow. I didn't mean to break the glass. It was such a small stone...." he said in an apologetic voice. "I just wanted her attention." Then, "Where's Sam?"

"Downstairs with the cousins," I said. "I have a problem." I looked out at the tree in front of Sam's room. "Think you can climb up and talk to me?"

He stared at me as if I were the one who was a werewolf. "Are you nuts?" He waved his crutch in the air. "I'm not dumb enough to do that twice."

I considered climbing down that tree, but seeing that crutch made me reconsider. The truth was, I was more likely to end up with a broken neck than a leg. Asking Cassie to drive me to the hospital wasn't an option.

I decided calling down to him was worth the risk of Sam and the cousins overhearing below. Fingers crossed, they were all asleep anyway.

"So..." This was kind of hard to explain. "Duke, I think Sam is in danger."

He moved closer to the bottom of the window. "Really?" His face was illuminated in the moonlight.

I blurted, "I think her cousin might be a werewolf."

He didn't start laughing, so that was a start. "What makes you think so?"

I was going to give him my list of clues but decided to go the direct route. I grabbed the journal and held it out so he could see it. "This book told me."

"Huh?"

I should have expected that.

"The Scaremaster is the author of the journal. His stories appear, then disappear."

"Go on," he said, still not laughing.

"The first story was about a girl, who thought she was rescuing a puppy, only it wasn't a dog at all. At the end, there was a big secret about it." I paused, gauging his reaction, and, when he didn't say anything, went on. "In this new story, the girl discovers it was a werewolf who bit her. The first time she transformed at a full moon, she prowled the neighborhood at night, terrorizing small animals, searching for prey. She didn't catch anything and went to bed hungry." I went on. "The next time she changed, her sister locked her into her room. When she snapped out of it the following morning, there was fresh blood on the carpet. No one could explain what had happened. One thing was sure: She wasn't hungry anymore." I shuddered. "She knows she's a wolf, but she can't remember what happens while she's transformed—which makes it all even more dangerous."

Retelling this was horrifying. The story was so eerie, I didn't really want to say it out loud, but I really needed Duke to believe me.

"There was a second chapter to this one," I told him. "It starts in the park—during a moonlit walk. Four girls are out, looking at the full moon. The girl transforms into the werewolf."

I knew which one but didn't say. Not yet.

"The werewolf chases everyone into a heavily wooded area, then corners them, one by one. First, the wolf bites her own cousin." I repeated the word "cousin" so he'd understand I was talking about Sam. "She instantly changes into a werewolf too. The other girl goes for help, but she never comes back."

I knew who that part referred to also. By the process of elimination, there was only one girl left. Not Sam. And not Cassie, who was the werewolf. That left Riley as the one who disappeared, because next was my part.

"Together, the two werewolf-cousins chase a girl called Emma into the basement." I couldn't see Duke's face clearly but could tell he was listening, so I went on. "I'm not kidding. The only girl with a name in the story is *me*." I leaned as far out the window as I could without falling and told him, "The whole story started 'Once upon a time, there was a girl named Emma....' " They all did. The Scaremaster wasn't very creative about the way his stories began.

Duke stared at me. "So...based on a story in a supposedly magical book starring girls with no names, you think Sam is in danger?"

When he put it that way, it did sound like something I was making up.

"I'm telling you, Duke—it's not a coincidence. I can easily guess the two girls are Sam and Riley and that the wolf is Cassie. Plus, the park sounds like the one nearby: trees on one side, playground on the other, with thick grass between." I had one last bit of evidence. "And the basement in the story is the exact same as the one in this house!"

"What happens to the girl in the basement?" he asked.

"It's awful," I said, closing my eyes to keep from crying. "The werewolf corners Emma, I mean me, under the single hanging lightbulb. I scream and scream, but no one comes to save me." My voice broke with the stress of it all.

That was the end.

In a long silence, I stared down at Duke. His face was pale in the light. He must have been afraid. I thought he'd go grab a weapon or something and rush back to help me.

But instead he said, "I saw that movie, Emma."

"What movie?" I was baffled.

"The one about the book and the stories."

"Huh? What are you talking about?"

"*Closer Encounters of a Different Kind.*" He said, "Funny joke, Emma. First you pelt me with oranges; then you try to sell me on some crazy story." Duke backed away from the window, limping as he went. "No more tricks. Tell Sam I'll pay for the window."

"Tricks?" I called after him. "What tricks?" I wasn't the tricky kind. Didn't he know that? Not even on April Fools' Day or Halloween. I NEVER PLAYED TRICKS!

Then again, I had screamed like a maniac when he came to the door earlier. With that in mind, I could see what he meant.

"Don't go," I begged. "I need you." I added, "I'll help you ask Sam to the dance!"

He didn't turn around.

"Please…" I added. "It's life or death." I tried one last thing. "Save me," I breathed. "This could be my last weekend ever."

I heard the distinct sound of Duke's back door shutting.

I was on my own.

Again.

I carefully shut the window and pulled down the blinds to make the room feel more safe and secure. Then I rushed down the stairs. Everyone was, as I expected, still asleep.

I lay down close to Sam, not in my sleeping bag, but on the floor next to her. I shook her shoulder. "Sam," I whispered in a throaty voice. "We gotta go." Where, I didn't know. But we had to leave! "Come on."

She didn't budge.

"Sam." My voice was a little louder. From the other side of me, Cassie snore-growled. "Wake up." I shook her harder.

She didn't even open one eye. It was like trying to wake the dead.

I scooted over to Riley. I'd start there instead.

"Riley!" My voice was getting louder and louder as I became more desperate. "Get up." She rolled over, her back to me. "Come on, little friend." I tried to push her out of the sleeping bag. I was getting pretty aggressive now. It was like shoving a log. Same as Sam, she wasn't waking up—not for anything.

"Shhh…" The voice came from the next sleeping bag over. "Go back to sleep, Emma."

"I—" I'd been caught by Cassie. Of all people in the room, of course, she was the one who wasn't dead to the world. "Sorry," I whispered to her.

"You will be really sorry if you don't go back to sleep now," she grunted in a low, guttural voice.

I didn't say another word. Too terrified to do anything else, I crawled into my sleeping bag. I had twenty-four hours to figure out what to do.

Werewolf weekend was a nightmare come true. I lay in my sleeping bag and stared at the ceiling. I couldn't sleep.

Chapter Twelve

I woke up late. I don't know what happened, but I must have fallen asleep at some point. When I got up, it was noon! NOON!

Half the day was gone. I knew, according to Sam's schedule, that the moon was going to rise in about six hours. And I hadn't made any real plans to protect my friends. This was bad.

Feeling groggy and with my hair sticking up, I stumbled into the kitchen.

"Good morning, sleepyhead," Cassie said with a wicked grin. "I hope you don't want anything, because I just cleaned up. If you're hungry, you should probably go home." The way she said it would have sounded like she was joking, but I knew better.

I gave her a long look that said "I thought we settled this. No way. Nohow."

No matter how awesome Sam thought her

cousin was, I was never going to like her. I already had plans to haunt Cassie for the rest of her life if she mauled me, Sam, and Riley tonight. I'd rattle those chains she had down by the cage....

"Why didn't you wake me?" I asked Sam.

"You were snoring so peacefully," she said. Her hair was so high and fluffy—it was poised for the best day ever. For me, the way things were going, it would be the worst. Even if we lived through the night.

"Get dressed, Emma!" Riley said. "We're about to build the telescope!" She grabbed my hand. "Let's go upstairs. I'll help you pick your outfit."

I didn't want to leave Sam alone with Cassie, but the sun was up and that felt sort of safe, so I went.

Riley picked a dress for me. It wasn't one I'd packed. It was Sam's, but I'd worn it before and was sure she wouldn't mind.

"I look kind of fancy," I told Riley as I checked out the knit green sweaterdress, paired with boots and a yellow-checkered scarf. "Is this too much for today?"

"You look fabulous," Riley said, admiring her work. I could see she was considering what to do about my tangled mop of morning hair. "It's a celebration."

I don't know why the idea of celebrating the

full moon put me over the edge at that minute, but I snapped.

"It's too dangerous to go out tonight," I told her. "The celebration is canceled."

All that work I had done to bring Riley back to being a friend was ruined in an outburst of stress and frustration.

She stared at my messy hair as if I was hopeless. "Why do you have to ruin everything?!" Riley stomped out of the room.

I chased her down in the hall and caught up by the bathroom.

"I just want to keep you safe," I explained. "Full moons bring out werewolves."

"DUH! Like I didn't know that!" she shouted, then dashed down the steps faster than I could keep up. As she leapt down the last stair, I heard her exclaim, "I hate the moon!"

I got to the kitchen as fast as I could. Moon pie creation, in preparation for the "celebration" that I'd just declared canceled, was in full swing. Sam had bits of white flour in her hair, and Cassie was wearing the apron from the night before. Now that I was taking a good look, they'd both clearly been styled by Riley.

Cassie was wearing new black clothes, but her hair was swept into a long braid. There was a black ribbon tied at the end, a sure indication of Riley's touch.

Like me, Sam was in a dress. Only hers was a frilly party dress. I almost laughed. We'd gotten that one together for the sixth-grade dinner, and it didn't really fit her anymore. I kept my giggle inside. There were more serious things pressing.

Riley was sitting on a stool at the counter, giving me the stink eye. Her look told me she hadn't shared what happened upstairs, but if I made one wrong move, she would get me rebanished for the rest of the weekend.

I mouthed that I was sorry. If I was going to make sure everyone lived through the night, I really needed to get a grip.

Riley glared at me for a heartbeat. I couldn't tell if she accepted the apology because she turned her head away and gave a silent signal to Cassie. Her sister nodded, and the two of them left the kitchen to talk privately.

I waited till they were in the other room, then moved in that direction. I had to hear what was going on. I hoped they were talking about the cage.

I'd reviewed the purpose of the jail cell in the basement a million times in my head and was starting to think of ways to use it. Should we lock ourselves in for our safety? Or should we lock Cassie in—also for our safety?

Cassie had clearly built it for someone to be held inside, but I still hadn't determined who. I planned to ask the Scaremaster, but to do that, I would have to go upstairs, and I wasn't leaving Sam again until I absolutely knew she'd be safe without me.

Sam was stirring the moon pie mixture and humming. I stationed myself in a place I could still see her and strained to hear what Cassie and Riley were saying.

"That's what Emma said," I heard Riley tell her sister.

"Emma is right," Cassie replied.

Okay, so it wasn't about the cage, but it was equally bizarre. Me? I was right about what?!

"I can handle it," Riley was whining. "Nothing bad will happen."

"No," Cassie replied. "It's too dangerous."

"Mom and Dad would say it's all right," Riley said.

"No they wouldn't," Cassie replied. "They'd keep the secret."

The Scaremaster's first story, the one that had gotten me in so much trouble, was playing out in the living room! Cassie did have a secret. And Riley knew what it was! They were whispering. This was terrible.

I remembered what the story had said. I am not sure why I hadn't mentioned it before, but there were details in there that I couldn't have known. That is, if they were true. And many things that didn't make sense. Plus, there was that terrifying line: *Emma must be stopped....*

Oh no!

"Whatcha doing?" Sam said, coming to stand by me.

On impulse, I turned to her. "Shhh."

"Are you eavesdropping on my cousins?" Sam asked, eyes wide. "You wouldn't do that, would you, Emma?"

I shook my head. "No," I said. "I..." Even in my ever-creative spinning mind, there was no excuse I could come up with fast enough. "So, yes," I admitted. "I was listening." I quickly went on. "Sam, Cassie is a werewolf. We can't go out with her tonight. The moon is going to make bad stuff happen."

"You're losing your mind," Sam said. "Stop it right now."

"Fine," I gave in, but it was going to be on my terms. "I'll stop, but you have to stay right next to me. All day and night."

"No way," Sam said firmly. "If I have to go to the bathroom, I'm going alone. If I need something upstairs, I'm going—"

"Fine," I cut her off, both as a distraction and because I'd forgotten to tell her something important. "But if you do go upstairs, don't freak out about the window."

She'd already been upstairs earlier to change clothes, but I guess she hadn't noticed since I'd closed the blinds.

"What?!" Sam stormed past me to the stairs. "What did you do, Emma?"

"Nothing," I said, "I promise. Pinkie-promise. It wasn't me." I stuck to her like glue as she entered her bedroom.

I shouldn't have said anything, because once she pulled up the slats, she went ballistic. I swear I could feel Sam's shocked reaction resonate in my own bones when she saw the window. "What happened?" she asked, voice tight.

I sounded like a five-year-old when I said, "Duke did it."

"No way," Sam said, hands on hips. "What really happened, Emma?"

"Duke," I repeated. "He threw a rock at the window to get your attention." I decided to give him a little rescue. "He likes you. And just wanted to talk to you. Isn't that sweet?"

"I don't know why you keep lying to me," Sam said.

"I'm not lying." I crossed my heart with a finger. "On my honor." I looked around for the rock, but I couldn't find it. It had probably rolled under the bed or fallen into a corner.

"You have to tell my parents," Sam said, storming back out of the room. "You broke it; you get to explain." She went back downstairs, with me on her heels.

"Oh, Sam, there you are," Cassie said as we entered the living room. "There was a delivery." She smiled at me, and my stomach sank. "The zombie kid next door stopped by."

"A delivery? From Duke?" Sam looked at Cassie, then looked at me.

Cassie held out a small box.

"For me?" Sam asked, reaching forward.

Cassie pulled the little red box away. "No," she said. "It's for Emma." She thrust the box at me as Sam stepped back.

"That doesn't make sense," I said. "Are you sure?"

"He was muttering, but I am almost positive he said 'Emma.'" Cassie turned to Riley, who confirmed it.

I took the box and very slowly lifted the lid. "Oh, Duke." I sighed as I raised a thin silver chain out of the box. There was a pendant on the end. A small matching silver ball about the size of a marble.

I saw Cassie's eyes widen in surprise, but she recovered quickly.

"Ha!" Sam said. "This proves you broke the window. Your story doesn't hold up. Duke didn't throw a rock to get *my* attention. If there was a rock, and I'm not saying there was without proof, it was to get *your* attention. So you are responsible for the damage either way." She pointed at the necklace in my hand. "He doesn't like me.... Obviously, he likes you!"

"He doesn't like me," I said to her. "He's teasing me."

Sam shook her head, then twirled in her too-tight dress. "You can borrow this beautiful gown when you two get married."

"And I'll do your hair," Riley added, as if all was forgotten. It seemed that the hysterical idea that I was marrying Duke, while we were still in middle school, was enough for everyone to forgive what had happened earlier.

Plans were made for my color scheme and my dress and my flowers and my hair while we finished the moon pie and built the telescope. Cassie and Sam were my bridesmaids, and Riley was the flower girl.

With Sam's love of schedules, I was surprised she didn't mark it all down on a calendar.

"Uh, I'm twelve years old," I interjected for the zillionth time. "And Duke likes Sam, not me." But they didn't care. They were all having fun.

I didn't get offended; first, because I knew they were just fooling around, but more than that, no one seemed mad at me anymore. We were together, and that was what was important.

Truth was, I knew what was in Duke's head, and it wasn't a matchup with me.

Silver is the one thing that is rumored to keep

away werewolves. I didn't need a movie or an old leather journal to tell me that. It was a myth, like a stake to the heart for a vampire or a bucket of water tossed on the Wicked Witch of the West.

Werewolves were afraid of silver because it was the one thing that could kill them. A silver bullet to the heart was the only effective weapon against a werewolf, so for self-preservation, they instinctively backed away from all things silver.

I'd told Duke about the werewolf, and he, through this present, was mocking me.

Even though it was a joke, I decided to wear the necklace, just in case. I slipped the chain over my head and let the silver marble rest against my shirt.

The day passed faster than I could have imagined. Cassie only told me to leave like ten times. Each time she did, I stuck closer to Sam.

Sometime around dinner, Cassie gave up and stopped nagging at me and casting evil looks.

"Let the festivities begin!" Sam announced the instant the sun began to dip below the horizon.

This whole thing was bound to an atomic clock she had found online. Sunset was minutes away.

While the sun went down, Sam took her time packing a backpack with the telescope and moon pies she'd made earlier.

I didn't want to leave her alone for even one second, but I'd known all day that there was something I had to do. This was the first opening I'd gotten.

I considered forcing her to wear Duke's silver pendant while I was away, but she'd never go for it. I'd simply have to hurry.

I was tense, but this was important. I needed one last conversation with the Scaremaster.

When Sam told everyone to get their jackets, I said, "Mine's upstairs," and took off two steps at a time.

I didn't even turn on the light in Sam's room. The rising moon was plenty bright to read by.

I flipped open the leather journal. There on the first page, the Scaremaster had written exactly what Sam had said: *Let the festivities begin*. My heart pounded, and I got a serious case of the chills.

I felt so nervous that my hands were shaking as I wrote down my question:

What's the cage for?

I needed to know, did we go in it or not? That would determine my next move.

The Scaremaster answered right away.

There's no cage in the story.

I considered that, mentally reviewing the narrative in my head.

It was true. No cage. Just me and a snarling werewolf in the basement. Until the point where there was no me anymore.

Hmmm. I considered what this discovery meant, but I had no answer.

I tried the Scaremaster again:

Someone needs to be locked inside it for safety. Cassie or us?

Stop meddling, Emma.
I am warning you.

I felt feisty. And mad. I wrote in firm letters:

Don't threaten me.

The story will unfold the way I wrote it.

I thought back to the ending the Scaremaster had written. Shivers went through my entire body, head to toes. I shook the pen to get as much ink as I could in the tip and scribbled:

I am a better writer than you.
THIS STORY IS ABOUT TO CHANGE!

Then, before the Scaremaster could reply, I shut the book and tossed it under Sam's bed. Me and the Scaremaster were done. This night was NOT going to go his way.

I would stop him.

Chapter Thirteen

We were heading to the park.

Since that was where the Scaremaster's story began, I tried desperately to convince Sam that we should avoid going there. First step to change the story—change the setting.

"The schedule says park," Sam told me on the way. "I planned everything to happen in the park. Therefore, we are going to the park."

Ack. Why did she have to be so, so…Sam! It was infuriating.

I gave up. But then, to my complete shock, Cassie said, "Yeah. The park's a bad idea."

I nearly fell over, I was so surprised. "What?" I said, turning to her.

"I'm just agreeing," she said to me. I remembered that she'd told Riley I was "right" when they'd had their private meeting off the kitchen. I couldn't mention that, however, without letting her know I had been eavesdropping, which I'd never, ever admit.

So Cassie didn't want to go to the park.... Interesting.

Her declaration totally threw me off. For the Scaremaster's story to come true, we had to stay in the park. I figured, as the main character, she'd stick to the plot.

This was an unexpected twist.

"Let's hang around here," Cassie suggested. "Got any more Nature Channel documentaries?" she asked Sam.

I could see Sam almost fall for it.... Almost, but not. She did love those documentaries.

"I have some," Sam said at last. "But we can watch them tomorrow. Tonight, we're going to the park."

That's Sam. Once she has a plan, it's nearly impossible to alter it.

Cassie bit the inside of her lip. "Okay, fine." She gave in, but the whole thing was still baffling. What was she up to?

Until I had this all figured out, I was going to have to go along and improvise as I went. I had this big idea that every time I could change a detail in the story, I would. It wasn't a great plan, but that's how stories work. Change one thing, and everything else was going to change too. Like if I had gone with Sam to get the stuff for the telescope, I wouldn't have the journal. Or if Mrs. L's ferret hadn't been sick, I wouldn't be here right now, scared to death, flipping out, heart thumping.

I hoped that a bunch of small changes put together would add up to us all living through the night.

At the park, Sam set up the telescope in the exact same grassy spot the Scaremaster had described. I couldn't even get Sam to move it three feet left. She was so stubborn!

I needed something else.

"We'll look at the moon for a while," she told us all. "Then start walking around at exactly midnight." Sam waved a printed map. "I have the best viewing sites marked according to longitude and latitude, and maximized to avoid big trees that might block our view."

I wondered if I could convince her to start the walk at 11:52. I didn't know. That one thing might make all the difference in the world.

Sam wasn't cooperating. She had a short lecture

scheduled, which was timed to end around midnight. "There are thirty thousand visible craters, and the largest on the visible side is called Bailly," she began.

By the way that Cassie yawned and Riley rolled her eyes, I knew they were not interested in any of this at all. Sam was oblivious. She was in her groove, going on about the dimensions of the Bailly crater.

After the lecture, we ate the celebratory moon pies and sat for a little while in the light of the moon while Sam explained how the ocean tides were linked to the moon's phases.

I could barely hear her. I kept staring at Cassie, waiting for her to grow fuzz on her face. Or start howling. So far, it was nearly midnight, and the Scaremaster's story was still on track.

Unsure what I was going to do when Cassie finally transformed, I eyed the park for escape routes. Any direction except through the dense trees would be a change. Maybe if we hid from the werewolf under the playground slide, it would be enough to shift the Scaremaster's ending.

Suddenly, Cassie said, "It's practically midnight. We have to go back to the house."

Here we go again. What was going on? Cassie wanted to leave?! Nothing made sense.

"It's not midnight yet," Sam countered. "We are starting the moonlit walk exactly at midnight." She tapped the face of her watch.

"Can't do it." Cassie rubbed her eyes. "Long day. I'm beat." She put her arm around Riley, in an aggressive way, as if holding Riley in place. "Riley shouldn't stay up so late, Sam. She's too young." There was another of those strange glances I'd seen between them.

Sam began her counterarguments. "We don't get to see each other very often, and the full moon only rises every 29.53 days. We don't have very long to wait, and I planned to talk about a few more craters." She gave begging eyes to Cassie. "Come on, Cassie. Let's stay out. Just this once."

Riley imitated Sam's eyes and echoed, "Come on, Cassie. Just this once? It's a celebration. It'll be okay."

"No." Cassie was firm. Her grip on Riley tightened. "I already told you the moonlit walk was a bad idea." She turned to Sam. "We need to go to the house."

"You can't cancel the walk." That was probably

the strangest thing I'd ever said. I was the one who had wanted to cancel the whole night! But now that we were here, the park seemed safer than the house. It was bigger with more places to run and hide. I figured that if we fled left instead of right, like in the story, it might be enough to save us all. And if Cassie wanted to be in the house, it was definitely a place I *didn't* want us to be!

"I'm in charge. We're leaving," Cassie said firmly.

In my head, I could hear the Scaremaster laughing at this unexpected development. It would benefit him if we went to Sam's house. It was much easier to fulfill the nightmare in the story, if we were in the house with no way to escape. At the house, the werewolf could have three victims instead of just one.

This was not the change the story needed.

"Come on, Riley," Cassie said. Then to my horror, she added softly, "We're going to Sam's basement."

Whoa! What? The basement?!

I had no doubt that the Scaremaster was behind Cassie's decisions. He somehow knew what I was doing and was bending the story to go his way.

It was a battle to "The End."

If I wanted a new ending, it was time for me to create one. Now or never!

I rushed forward. My adrenaline was pumping. I felt like a superhero flying in to the rescue. I snatched Riley out from under Cassie's arm and shouted to Sam, "Run!"

"Huh?" Riley was confused, but I gripped her hand tight in mine. "We have to get away. Before it's too late!" I shrieked at Sam to follow us left toward the park's playground. My voice echoed in the dark, cool air. "We have to stick together!"

Cassie leapt forward. In the dark, it looked more like a dog's leap than a human one. She tackled me to the ground. "You don't know what you're talking about, Emma!"

"Yes I do!" I countered. I cast my eyes toward Sam. "Take Riley away. Far away."

Cassie was sitting on me now, teeth bared. "Go ahead, bite me! I'll sacrifice myself if you leave Sam and Riley alone," I offered.

Sam and Riley backed away, but they didn't run. It was most likely because I was thrashing around and they didn't want to get hurt. Cassie was strong, but I was determined to save my friends.

I kneed her in the chest and made a wild karate chop to the side of her arm. It was pathetic, but enough to shock her. I managed to push her off me and struggled to stand.

Once I was on my feet, I took off toward Riley, snagging her hand once more. "Come on!" I tugged. "We gotta get away!"

"Riley, you need to come with me!" Cassie told her sister. She didn't try to fight me again, instead keeping safely away from my weapon-like hands. "Hurry. There's no time left," she pleaded.

"I'll protect you," I told Riley. She must have been really nervous because her hand was warm and slippery in mine.

"It's happening, Cassie," Riley called over her shoulder as I dragged her away, not realizing that I was turned around, going the wrong way. I was in such a frantic state, I didn't realize which way I was heading until it was too late. We'd entered the wooded part of the park, putting the Scaremaster's story back on track.

I heard Cassie shout, "I'll get help!"

I ran and ran and ran, dragging Riley along behind me. When we came to the deepest, wooded part of the park, I finally stopped to rest. We were both out of breath and panting hard.

We were alone.

Noting that the full moon was directly overhead, I felt a rush of defeat.

It was midnight.

I had failed at my one goal. I'd left Sam with her cousin. Now Sam was with Cassie, primed to be bitten and transformed into a werewolf.

I was devastated.

If I couldn't save Sam, I was determined to keep Riley nearby. No matter the tricks the Scaremaster played, this little girl would not "disappear" on my watch.

Under a shady tree where the moonlight didn't shine, I tightened my fingers around her palm.

"Ouch!" I screamed, and pulled away as the hand I held scratched me with razor-sharp nails. I looked over just in time to see Riley sink down onto all fours on the leaf-covered forest floor.

"Get out of the way, Emma!" Cassie appeared just then. She shoved me to the side. The moon had moved slightly, and now, I could see red specks of blood forming across my palm where Riley had scratched me.

Cassie shouted, "I knew from the minute I saw you on the driveway that you'd cause problems!" She frantically looked over her shoulder at Sam, who was very much still human. "We have to get Riley to your basement! Don't ask questions. Just help!"

Sam was so stunned, she was frozen as if paralyzed. Everything she knew to be true about science and biology and human nature had just been thrown out the window. Her brain was slowly processing it all. Too slowly.

She and Riley were face-to-face.

Riley, or the werewolf that used to be Riley, was staring at Sam through hungry wolf eyes. She was panting and gnashing her jaw.

The outfit Riley had spent so much time picking for the moon celebration was in tatters on the ground. Matted fur covered her skin. It wasn't her fingernails that had scratched me—it was her sharp claws. Her jaw was wet, and her sharp fangs glistened in the moonlight.

Riley howled at the moon.

If Sam didn't move, I knew what was coming next. I'd read the story.

We stood there for a heartbeat.

This was all wrong. I couldn't let the Scaremaster win, but what else could we do?

"I tried to get Riley to the basement," Cassie said. There was an edge to her tone that seemed to imply this was all my fault. "The cage belongs to her."

Yeah, I got that now. There was no time to apologize or talk about how we'd reached this point. I still knew in my heart that we had to change the story, but how? Was it too late?

The wolf snarled at Sam and moved in closer.

If Sam got bitten, the Scaremaster's horrible story would unfold.

"Hey, little wolf." A voice came from behind us. "I have a treat for you."

Wait. That wasn't in the story. For a heartbeat, I turned away from Riley and Sam to see who was there.

"Duke." It was Sam who breathed his name.

"I heard Cassie calling for me to help," he said. "Even though she explained, I didn't expect to find this." His crutches glinted in the moonlight.

"I knew from his gift to Emma that Duke had read a lot about werewolves," Cassie said, giving me a sideways glance. "Plus, he's the only other person in town I know."

I remembered he said he'd seen the movie Riley loved. "Fan of the supernatural?" I asked.

"You know it." He grinned in the moonlight. "Did I tell you my new house is haunted? I'm a lucky guy." Duke sounded more confident and assured than I'd ever heard. He didn't seem surprised to find out that werewolves actually existed or that there was one standing in the local park. "Sorry for not believing you before, Emma. After the orange thing…well, I thought you were just trying to trick me. Now let's get this puppy to the basement."

I was so relieved he was there, even though part of me doubted how a guy with a broken leg could really help.

In a flash, something really important dawned on me. In the story, there was no one else besides us in the park. Now Duke was here. That meant the story was changing.

And: Cassie had gone for help, and unlike in the story, she hadn't disappeared. She had come back!

Another thing: I realized, there was a *cage* in the basement.

The Scaremaster had warned me that it wasn't

part of his story, but I didn't understand what he meant. Now I did.

Cassie had begun to change the story before I even understood it needed to be changed.

It was suddenly obvious: The Scaremaster hadn't written a cage in the original gruesome tale because he knew, if Riley was behind bars, we'd all be safe from her AND she'd be safe from hurting herself or anyone else. The cage was for everyone's protection. But the Scaremaster didn't want me to think of it.

I smacked my forehead. I wished I had figured it all out earlier.

Little things were happening. But if we were going to survive the night, we still needed more little things.

"Bring a weapon?" I asked Duke.

"Emma!" Cassie snapped at me. "No weapons. We don't want to hurt her. She's just a little girl."

I looked at Riley, who had begun circling around Sam, eyes flashing, stalking her prey.

"She's a werewolf," I said.

"We aren't hurting my cousin," Sam called to us. The werewolf was inches away and a heartbeat from pouncing on her neck. "Come up with something else."

"Did you bring a dog leash?" I asked Duke.

"No." He threw something at me. "Here. Try this."

I reached out to catch whatever he had tossed, but missed. It sailed over my head, falling just behind me. I turned to get it, but the wolf lunged past me and got there first. She devoured the thing in a single bite, wrapper and all, before crawling back toward Sam.

"Whew. That's good news. She likes granola bars," he said with a half shrug. "I was rushing out so fast, I tried to grab something ten-year-old girls like. Werewolves might be scary, but she's still human underneath all that fur."

I wished I had caught the granola bar. Maybe we could have broken it into pieces and used it as a lure.

Lure...

Okay, so I didn't have any food to bring her along, but I had something that was supposed to keep werewolves away. I lifted the chain Duke had given me as a joke from my neck and quickly peeled off the small silver ball.

I had about a second to make the throw of my lifetime.

"Sam, catch!" I tossed it in the air.

My throw was wobbly, but in the same instant that Riley leapt toward her, Sam caught the silver orb. She held it out in front of Riley.

The wolf, seeing the shining glint of the silver, recognized it as something she had to stay away from. She sank to the earth and immediately backed away.

Sam was safe, for the time being, but the werewolf's craving was still strong. She turned her attention to Duke. It wasn't slow stalking anymore. She was on the prowl, hungry and determined. It was only a matter of minutes before she struck, transforming our classmate and neighbor into a monster.

"Duke, watch out," I warned.

I could hear the low, hungry growl in Riley's throat as she crept forward.

"Sam," he said, through tight lips. "Toss me the silver ball."

She threw it. He caught it, and the werewolf backed away, setting her sights on Cassie.

"I have an idea," Cassie said as her own sister

moved in for a vicious bite. "I'll start moving backward toward the house. When she gets close to me, throw me the pendant."

"Whoever she is chasing can get her to follow." I was on it. "Then we toss the pendant for protection."

This was a slow way to get from the park to the house. But it was another change. There was no silver pendant in the Scaremaster's book. Based on that fact alone, I knew it would work.

Cassie moved back pretty far, with her sister dangerously stalking her. Duke passed her the ball, and the danger shifted to me.

I'd thrown it once, and it worked out for Sam. But now I had to catch.

If I missed, I was going to become a werewolf. Or worse—a werewolf's midnight snack.

I glanced up to the sky and sent a silent wish to the mythological Man in the Moon. If he existed, now would be a good time to prove it. "Please let me catch the ball."

I took giant steps backward, letting Riley come very close. Her teeth were bared, and I could see the drool beneath her jaw. My hand ached where she'd clawed at me.

I made it to the end of Sam's driveway, when Cassie threw me the protection amulet.

It soared toward me in slow motion. I saw it, shimmering as if it hung on a bright moonbeam. I reached out at the same time the werewolf pounced forward. Riley's sharp claws stabbed me in the shoulder blades. I was pinned to the ground.

Her face lowered. I could see the fangs that were about to puncture my neck. I could smell her breath, a mixture of musty wolf scent with moon pie and granola bar.

I stared the werewolf in the eyes, and then I opened my hand.

The silver ball sparkled in her golden eyes. Sensing her own life in jeopardy, she backed away.

My blood was pumping so fast, I thought I was having a stroke. I couldn't breathe. I eventually threw the pendant to Duke, then laid there on the driveway while Cassie and Duke worked together to move Riley into the house and toward the basement.

Sam came and stood over me. "You okay?" she asked.

It took me a minute to answer. I nodded and managed to gasp out, "Can you move a little? You're blocking my view." Sam stepped back. I stared up to the sky and silently thanked the Man in the Moon. I swear I saw him wink.

When we caught up with the others, Werewolf Riley was at the bottom of the basement stairs. Duke had the silver pendant. I motioned for him to switch places with me and to give me the pendant.

"I have something else for you," Duke said. He pulled another granola bar out of his coat pocket. He passed it over. "Let's finish this."

The last toss was up to me. I imagined where I wanted that bar to land. Taking off the wrapper this time, I took a deep breath, focused, and threw.

"Bull's-eye!" I cheered as it fell exactly in the center of the cage floor.

For a long moment, Riley stood outside the bars, looking in.

We all started to back away into the dimly lit corner with the single lightbulb. If this didn't work, we were back to the place where the Scaremaster wanted us.

The swinging lightbulb cast shadows on the narrow stairs to the living room. Four of us running at once, it was impossible that we'd all escape.

Riley looked at each of us in turn. Then she let out a mighty howl. Louder and stronger than any we'd heard before. Lowering her head, she walked into the cage.

Cassie closed the cage door behind her and chained it tight.

We all watched Riley devour the granola bar in a single gulp. She paced the cage, as if searching for more food but, realizing there was none, gave up and sat down. She turned around a few times, pawed at the ground, then sank to the floor. With a long last howl, Cousin Riley curled up in a ball and went to sleep.

We gathered and hugged one another.

Then there were the "sorry"s.

We all sat in the glow of that single swinging lightbulb and apologized to each other.

"I'm sorry I didn't believe you," Sam told me.

"I'm sorry I didn't handle this better," I said. "And sorry I blamed you," I told Cassie.

"I'm sorry I didn't bring more granola bars," Duke said.

"I'm sorry I didn't tell you all what was going on," Cassie added. "And I'm sorry I tried to get Emma to go home."

It went on like that for a while until we started to get too tired to be sorry anymore.

Leaving Riley safely in the cage, we went upstairs and said good night.

Duke had one last thing to say before he went home. He said to Sam, "I'm sorry I broke the window."

I stood with Sam and Cassie by the front door, watching him cross the yard.

I smiled.

The best writer had finished the story.

We'd come to "The End."

Chapter Fourteen

"You know what? I'm going to try out for the softball team," I told Sam when we woke up the next morning. We were lying in our sleeping bags, still wearing the clothes from the moon celebration. After Duke had gone home, we all crashed. It had been an exhausting weekend.

"I'm going to the winter dance with Duke," Sam said, rolling on her side to face me.

"Wait. What? He asked you?" I was shocked. "When?"

"Last night. Just before he left…" She blushed. "He said he'd been trying to ask, but it never went right."

I laughed. "Nothing like a little danger to bring us all together." I glanced toward the basement door. "And you're going to let Riley be your stylist?"

"Of course," Sam said. "She'll be really excited."

I leaned back into my pillow and asked, "Have you see her yet?"

"No." Sam sat up. "I heard Cassie get up hours ago. I bet they're together."

The sun was high in the sky. The danger had passed.

We got up and stumbled, lazy and still tired, into the kitchen.

"Breakfast is ready," Cassie told us, sweeping her arm toward a beautifully set table. She was wearing the flowered apron.

Riley was sitting at the table. "Hi," she said with a grin. "Look at us. We all survived another full moon. I wish Cassie would let me stay out! It's totally safe." She seemed to know she transformed but forgot what happened when she was a wolf. We all exchanged glances in a silent agreement not to tell her.

Cassie set a casserole dish on the table. With dramatic flair, she swept back the lid. The dish was filled with granola bars.

"These are from Duke." Cassie giggled. It was nice to see this side of her again. I liked her so much better when I wasn't suspicious and she wasn't creepy. She put her hand on Riley's head. "I have a strong feeling you'll love them."

"YUM!" Riley said, grabbing one and ripping off the wrapper.

I smiled. Then I jumped. And gasped.

"What?!" Sam stood up so fast, she knocked back her chair.

"AUGH!" I pointed at the back door and shrieked, "Zombie!"

The look on Sam's face was so full of terror that I laughed until I cried.

"It might take me awhile to get used to the fact that werewolves actually exist," Sam admitted, rolling her eyes at me. She went to let Duke come in while Cassie pulled up an extra chair.

When we all sat down, Cassie said, "I thought I could get through the night without telling Sam what was going on."

"I'd have never believed you anyway," Sam said.

"You could have told me," I put in. "I'd have believed you." To be honest, I don't know what I would have believed. There was no way to be sure. The Scaremaster and his possessed journal had put me on edge even before I'd arrived for the weekend.

I remember that feeling in my gut as if I was waiting for something to happen. And then it did.

Cassie gave a small snort. "I didn't want to tell you, Emma. This is a secret. A *family* secret."

"Not anymore," I said, glancing at all the faces around the table. Duke shrugged.

"Yeah," Cassie said. She stood up and got a knife from the kitchen. "That's why we have to make a blood pact never to tell. Riley's secret has to stay in this room." She held out the kitchen knife. The blade glinted. "Who wants to be the first to promise?"

My heart skipped two beats. I got up and backed away from the table. "I'm not cutting myself to..." Then I realized she was kidding. "I guess I'm still wound up," I admitted, knowing it was true because there was one last thing I had to deal with before the weekend ended.

Cassie put down the knife with a laugh. "Not blood. But we do need to make a pact."

"Be right back." Sam dashed from the room and came back a minute later with her telescope. "We swear on the moon to keep what happened here this weekend a secret." She set it upright in the middle of the table and wrapped her hand around the bottom.

I put my hand directly above hers and closed my fingers tight.

Duke went next, followed by Cassie and Riley. The telescope transformed into a pillar of promises.

Riley said, "This secret is between the five of us and the Man in the Moon."

We all agreed, and the pact was sealed.

I never had a better breakfast. The granola bars were delicious, and Cassie had made fruit salad and mini pancakes as well. Plus, we still had a few of the zombie's original donuts.

As we finished up, Sam said, "The adults won't be here for a few hours. What should we do?"

"Can we watch the movie again?" Riley asked. I realized she was already dressed for the day in clean, new clothes. Cassie must have made sure she had something to wear when she transitioned back.

Sam's eyes lit up. "The moon documentary?" She was excited. "Great idea!" Looking at me, she added, "You missed the whole first half."

Riley shook her head. "Not the moon one. My movie."

"Oh." Sam's face fell, but she agreed. "Okay. Emma missed part of that one too."

We piled on the couch. Before sitting down, I took off the silver chain and handed the pendant back to Duke. "Funny gift," I said. "Very useful too. But we don't need it anymore."

"Silver works against vampires too," he said, giving it right back to me.

With a laugh, I said, "I guess I should keep it, then. You never know." I fastened it back around my neck.

"I'll get Sam one too," Duke said. "Just in case." He winked. As an added note, Duke said to me and Sam, "Oh, hey, I've been meaning to say thanks. My grandpa said you found Maggie. He loves that dog."

Sam and I stared at each other for a long beat. We both laughed at the connection, but it made me feel unsettled. Again. There was something more to all these coincidences that sat like a stone in my belly.

Mom's work schedule, the lost puppy at school, the mysterious new librarian who wasn't our librarian at all, Mrs. L and the sick ferret, me coming to Sam's, Riley's secret, what happened in the park, even the fact that the reunion weekend was over a full moon... There could no longer be any doubt.

EVERYTHING was connected, and somehow, the Scaremaster had been lurking at every step.

We'd outsmarted him, though, and I didn't think he expected it. I also didn't think he was the type to give up so easily.

The movie started, and this time, I paid attention. Riley had said that the journal was in the movie. Duke had said he'd seen "that movie" when I described the Scaremaster's book. I had no idea what they meant, but I was determined to find out.

To my surprise, the book was briefly, casually mentioned in every interview. But it wasn't really discussed until the zombie part. I leaned up in my seat and remained focused while a girl talked about how she'd found a journal in her locker but knew it wasn't hers. She'd kept it anyway and discovered that there was a story in that book that came true!

The interview went on and on about the zombie, never going back to discuss the book's role in the drama. I might have not even paid attention to the few sentences about the mysterious book if I hadn't been looking for it or if I hadn't been warned it was there.

"Do you want to show us the journal?" Duke asked when the film ended.

"We should fully investigate," Sam said. "Maybe run some chemical tests on the composition of the paper to see if we can identify the source."

I really didn't want to touch that thing ever, but that wasn't an option. The weekend wasn't really over till the Scaremaster was silenced. Maybe if we worked together, we could destroy it once and for all.

I went upstairs and dumped out my overnight bag, searched under the bed, even rummaged through her closet.

The journal was gone.

Unfortunately, I knew where to find it.

When my mom came to pick me up, I thanked Sam for hosting me. I told Cassie and Riley I looked forward to seeing them again, which was the truth. And I gave a hug to Duke. His face turned red when I threw myself at him, but he had the rest of middle school and all of high school to get used to it. Now that we were friends, I planned to hug him a lot.

Mom talked about her trip the whole way home. The business was good, and she thought it might lead to a promotion.

It wasn't until we got into our apartment that Mom asked, "Anything interesting happen at Sam's?"

"Nah," I told her. "Just a plain ol' boring weekend."

Mom gave me a sideways glance. "Emma, remember after school on Friday? There was something you wanted to show me."

"Nope," I said. "It's all good." I told her I had homework and rushed into my room, closing the door behind me.

The journal was right where I expected it—back in my school backpack, just where I had left it.

I pulled it out and set it on my bed. For a long moment, I sat against my pillows, staring at the triangles on the cover, reflecting on the trouble the Scaremaster had caused. He had to be stopped.

I peeled back the cover. I expected a blank page and had an idea of what I wanted to write.

But the page wasn't blank.

The title, *Tales from the Scaremaster*, was there. And under that: *ACT II.*

ACT TWO?

I grabbed a pen and wrote.

One act was enough.

The reply appeared immediately.

Silly Emma. You thought you could beat me.

I drew in a breath as more words appeared.

The Scaremaster has many stories to tell.

I didn't reply. There was no use arguing with a possessed book.

Instead, I shut the cover and clasped it tight. I had to get rid of the Scaremaster's journal forever.

I was shaking when I went out to the dumpster. Fear set in. What if the story really did go on? It was too terrible to consider.

At Sam's, I'd tried to rip the journal pages, but they wouldn't tear. I'd pulled at the leather cover, but it held firm. So what were my options? Fire? Water? I needed something permanent.

When I came up with the answer, I dashed back into the house, flying past my mom as she called out, "What are you doing?"

"Recycling," I answered as I grabbed her sharpest crafting scissors.

"Good idea," she said when I dashed back past her, out the door, and down to the dumpster.

For the next half hour, I cut the journal pages. Every single one. I chopped them out of the book, then sliced them into little pieces.

There was a part of me that hoped that librarians everywhere would understand. I wasn't usually a destroyer of books. This one was special. This one had to go.

I made Scaremaster confetti and scattered it in the recycling bin.

The cover wouldn't cut, so I dug into the spine with my scissors. I was a little surprised how easily the thing ripped then and was fascinated that the book broke into two equal parts. I mean, exactly equal. I'd clearly hit the Scaremaster's weak spot.

Just to be completely sure the book was trash, I dug some long scratches into the leather cover to finish the job.

It was over. The journal would go out with the garbage, and that was the real end of the Scaremaster's story.

As I went back to the apartment, I pledged that from here forward I would no longer write horror stories.

I was going to try my hand at science fiction.

Epilogue

"This is your fault." Kaitlin Wang was furious. "You're always joking around, Noah!" She marched passed him on the way to the mess hall. "Someday, your pranks are going to get you in real trouble." She tucked her long brown hair under her Camp Redwood Vines cap, then looked at him over her shoulder. "When that happens, no one will be there to help you."

"Whatever," Noah muttered. It was only the first week of camp, and this was already his second trash assignment.

The first one he was by himself. It was just one afternoon. This time, Kaitlin was coming along. And it was for three whole days.

He wasn't going to apologize to her. It was her choice after all. Sort of.

Kaitlin didn't have to follow him to the boat dock. She didn't have to hide in the trees while he drilled nail holes in the Red cabin's kayak. And she certainly didn't have to turn him in to the counselors after his Blue cabin won the trophy.

Who did she think she was? Nancy Drew?

It was ironic that she had told on *him*, and they had gotten punished together.

According to Director Robinson, Kaitlin shouldn't have been out after curfew. Hers was a lesser crime, but still…a violation of camp rules.

Three days' mess duty was a second strike violation. "Poor" Kaitlin had gotten dragged down with him, even though it was her first offense—first probably in her whole life.

For the rest of the summer, Noah would have to gauge his pranks more carefully while watching over his shoulder for Kaitlin the Super Snoop.

Kaitlin stomped into the mess hall, letting the door slam before Noah came through. The wire screen reverberated with a bang, just barely missing his nose.

He sighed. Three days of trash duty with the one person who hated him most in the world seemed worse than being sent home. Then again, his parents were on a silent meditation retreat. He had nowhere to go but forward.…

Noah pulled open the screen door and stepped into the hot, sweaty kitchen. It was a hundred degrees outside. In the kitchen, it had to be double that. His dark mop of hair flattened and stuck to his forehead.

"Welcome, Noah." A young woman greeted him. Kaitlin was already standing next to her.

"Are you new?" Noah asked. This wasn't the same cook from Tuesday. That cook was a guy. With prison tattoos. Everyone called him Spike, though Noah was pretty sure that wasn't the name on his birth certificate.

For Spike, Noah had peeled hundreds of potatoes in addition to trash duty.

He wondered what torture this new cook had in mind.

"I've been around awhile," she answered. Her midnight-black hair glistened under the fluorescent lights. It was so dark it was practically purple. There was a glint in her golden eyes when she said, "There's so much to do. I need to start preparing dinner." She pointed through two double swinging saloon-type doors into the dining area. "You two should get started." She gave Noah a long, lingering look. "You know the drill."

"Trash, trash, trash," Kaitlin moaned, surveying the room. "There's always so much garbage at camp."

Campers were supposed to bus their own plates after meals. But there were always things left over: napkins, wrappers, paper cups. It was like they half cleaned and left the rest, knowing Noah would be there.

He sighed. The cook gave them each a pair of plastic gloves and a large white garbage bag. "When you are finished here, I have other tasks for you," she said. Her voice held an edge that Noah couldn't identify and he wondered what "other tasks" meant.

He didn't ask. It didn't matter. He was her prisoner for the next seventy-two hours. Noticing that she was grinning to herself in a secretive way, Noah watched as the cook disappeared back through the kitchen doors.

"You don't have much to say, eh, Noah?" Kaitlin asked as they walked around the edge of the mess hall collecting paper products and leftover food. "You're a sneaky guy, but not very chatty, huh?"

"Not to you," Noah retorted, snidely adding, "I don't know who you'll tell."

"That's not fair," Kaitlin countered. "I wasn't the one cheating to win the boat race."

"I wasn't the one who told on me." Noah was angry. Sure he'd cheated, but it was all in fun. Everyone had laughed when the team boat sank. No one was hurt; the campers simply swam back to shore. "It was funny!" he said.

"No, it wasn't," Kaitlin said. "You're lucky no one got hurt."

"There was no risk," Noah told her. "A good prankster knows how to keep it real." He gave her a small grin. "I'm a professional."

Kaitlin pulled up her plastic gloves and grabbed a half-eaten sandwich from the floor. As she dropped it in her trash bag, she said, "I want to be a reporter when I grow up. I'm always looking for a story. And I know, Noah Burns, that when you are around, something wild is going to happen."

Noah grabbed a paper cup off a table and tossed it at her head. "You're ruining my fun." It missed, landing softly on the floor by her foot.

Kaitlin picked up the cup and wadded it in a ball. She threw it back at him with such force and precision, it bounced off his forehead.

Kaitlin smiled. "You're looking at the captain of

the middle school tennis team and twelve-year-old regional Slam Jam basketball champion."

"La-di-da," Noah mocked. "I'm on the all-state improvisational comedy team." It wasn't true. He was up for the team, having made it through several rounds of tryouts, but his parents couldn't take him to the finals. They were too busy "finding themselves," as always.

The next hour passed in silence. He could see that Kaitlin wanted to talk but held her tongue. He wasn't very good at conversation anyway. It was better this way.

Just as they were finishing up, the new cook popped her head out of the kitchen. Her eyes had seemed gold when he'd first looked, but now they appeared brown or blue or...

Noah squinted at her. It might have been his imagination, but they kept changing.

"Trash dumpster is out back." She pointed toward the rear of the building. "After you're done here, come to the kitchen for your next assignment."

With a sigh, Kaitlin hefted her full, heavy bag and headed out. As she passed by Noah, he couldn't help himself—he reached out and snagged the baseball cap off her head.

"Hey." Kaitlin turned on a heel. "Give that back!"

Noah, acting on impulse, ran. He dashed around her, out the door, and around to the back of the dumpster.

She was fast and caught up easily. "Give me my hat." Kaitlin put a hand on one hip and stretched out the other.

"Go get it," Noah said, tossing her hat up and into the dumpster.

"I do not like you," she said. "Not even a little."

"I hear that all the time," he replied.

Kaitlin scowled at him as she hefted herself up and into the dumpster. She tossed out her hat and was about to climb back out when she announced, "Whoa. Hey, Noah. Check it out. I found an old book. There are these strange gash marks in the leather cover."

"A book?" Noah climbed up so he could peer into the dumpster. "Show me."

The discovery was so exciting, she seemed to have forgotten that a second ago she'd declared how much she didn't like him. Kaitlin stood in the dumpster, surrounded by bags of trash. "I think it's yours," she told Noah.

"I don't have a journal," he replied, adding, "Not my style."

"Then why is your name in it?" Kaitlin said with attitude, as if he was brain-dead. "Did you forget you wrote a story?" Rolling her eyes at him, she handed the leather-bound book over to Noah.

He opened the cover and read out loud:

Tales from the Scaremaster

Then below that, the story began....

Once upon a time, there was a boy named Noah....